CATFISH ALLEY

THE BARCELONOIR TRILOGY: BOOK 1

T. M. STRETTON

SPELLBOUND BOOKS

First Published by SpellBound Books 2023

for Danielle Fleet

Feros ferio

PART ONE
16—20 FEBRUARY 2014

DARK THERAPY

CHAPTER ONE

I'VE BEEN IN THE UNDERHEATED WAITING ROOM FOR NEARLY TWO hours. Standard institutional chic, puke-coloured, lino, plastic wood chairs bolted to the floor, posters curling away from tatty pinboards, and a vending machine I can't use because the change in my pocket comes to less than a euro. A smell of plastic and overcooked vegetables coming through the vents and a sub-audible electrical drone that I can feel rather than hear. Who'd have thought it? Thirty-two years old, a background like mine, and this is my first time in a police station.

The woman before me, a snooty English tourist who'd spent the previous half-hour indulging in lazy denunciations of the Spanish, has been in the interview room for longer than I'd expected. I thought she'd be out with a flea in her ear by now, but no such luck.

Eventually the door opens. She stalks out, heels clacking on the lino, throwing a "thanks for nothing" over her shoulder.

She's followed by a young female cop in a dark blue local police uniform, who puts her head round the door.

"Senyor Chisholm?"

I'm the only man left in the waiting room so she doesn't

need to be a detective to work out that's me. I get up and follow her in. She looks tetchy and tired as she sits behind a desk with a computer terminal and a pad of paper. I can't imagine the previous interview has put her in a better mood.

She indicates a plastic chair in front of her desk and I sit down. She clicks a leaky ballpoint and I see the ink stains on her fingers. Her badge says '12226'.

"I'd like to report a robbery," I say in Catalan. "My wallet was stolen on Rambla de Santa Mònica. Pickpockets."

She's surprised into a smile at my accent, which she quickly suppresses.

"I speak English," she says. Two years, and although my Spanish is good, I haven't cracked Catalan yet. "I'm sorry. The computers are down, so we will need to use paper."

"OK," I say. "I'm not in a hurry, take your time." With no cash it's not as if I have much else to do today.

"Your full name?" she says, pen poised.

"Thomas William Chisholm." I spell the surname, which has baffled locals ever since I moved to Barcelona.

"Your profession?"

"Writer." It sounds better than *bum*, which would be more accurate.

"You are a tourist?" she asks as she writes it down.

I shake my head. "No, I'm Scottish—British—but I live in Gràcia."

She looks up at me from her paperwork. Her deep brown eyes have a flicker of interest. "Residents are usually more careful. It's normally tourists who get robbed."

"Like the woman before me."

She sighs and purses her lips. I grin at her.

"I'm not going to give you a hard time. Not all of us are like her," I say. "This is my own fault."

She spins the ballpoint in her fingers. “I have to fill in a form, give you a crime number. How did it happen?”

I shake my head ruefully. “You know the shell games on the street? Which cup is the ball under? I was watching that, a kid bumped into me. Two minutes later and I realise my wallet’s gone.”

She gives me a sympathetic smile. It’s a sign of how much all this has fucked me off that I’ve only just realised how pretty she is. I’m getting old.

“The Ramblas are the worst place for it,” she says. “It’s the oldest trick on the street.”

“I know. I should have been paying attention. Look, I’m sorry my stupidity has given you all this paperwork.”

She shrugs but her eyes are friendly.

“And what was in the wallet?”

“My Banco Santander card, my metro T-10 ticket, eighty euros in cash.” Actually sixty euros—my last sixty until I get paid—but it looks better to bump it up a bit.

“I will be honest,” she says. “Unless you are very lucky, you will never see the wallet again. Phone your bank, cancel the card. The cash and the metro ticket will be used already. I’m sorry.”

“I thought as much. I just need the crime number for the bank.”

“Nothing of sentimental value in the wallet? Family photographs? Personal documents?”

“I’m not the sentimental type,” I say.

Her mouth twitches as if she thinks I’m flirting with her. If I’d known today was going to turn out like this, I’d have shaved this morning.

She finishes writing, tears off the carbon copy and hands it to me. “That has your crime number,” she says with a smile. “I’m sorry I can’t be more help.”

"*Gràcies* anyway," I say.

"*De res*. You're welcome."

Is there a flicker of attraction there? If I hadn't just split up with Carmen I might be tempted to find out—that and the fact that I now have no money at all. I'm in no hurry to try and find a new girlfriend and I'm not sure I'd want to go out with a cop anyway. Call me old-fashioned, but I like to keep the law at arm's length.

We shake hands—hers is warm and dry—and hope that I've left her with a better impression of the British than her previous case.

Out on the street, it's started to rain a cold February Barcelona drizzle. Without my metro ticket, I turn up my jacket collar and set off for the hike to Gràcia.

Back at the flat, I'm cold and damp, and things are no better. The laptop battery has gone flat despite being plugged in overnight, and I jiggle the lead until I get a green light. I find the bank's website and of course I can't report the theft of my bank card online, which means probably an hour in a queue on their telephone 'hotline'. I also have two unread emails which promise nothing good.

I peer through the cracked laptop screen. The first is from my landlord, pointing out that I'm two months behind with my rent. This is hardly news, and perhaps I can stall him a bit longer with a sob story about my stolen wallet. The second email is going to be harder to fob off.

From: Polly Hunter <pollyhunter@stmarysagency.co.uk>

To: Tommy Chisholm <kilmarnocktom@gmail.com>
Subject: Progress/Advance

Hi Tommy

Sorry to contact you by email but your phone is disconnected. Have you changed your number? A couple of things – firstly I need you to sign some paperwork for US tax filing.

Are you still at:

Baixada del Silur, 27
08024 Barcelona?

Also I wanted to touch base with you on progress with the second novel. You'll remember that the contract with Kilpatrick & Robinson stipulated delivery of the first draft by 31 August last year? I have stalled them so far but they are now talking about repayment of the first instalment of the advance. I'm sure we can extend the deadline if we can sell a realistic delivery plan, but at the moment I can't tell them anything because I don't know anything.

I'm doing my best to fight your corner but I have to say this continued silence on your part is unprofessional. It's normal to have problems with a book, and I know second novels are especially difficult, but I can't help you if you won't talk to me.

. . .

Looking forward to hearing from you soon.

Kind regards
Polly

Fuck. Not a great day so far. It's not Polly's fault, she's only doing her job, and this has always been going to happen, but I'd hoped not quite yet. The manuscript isn't even six months late. Am I going to have to speak to Polly about it? Don't get me wrong, I like her and I've heard plenty of stories from writers with worse agents, but I don't fancy telling her that I've already spent the advance, written not a single word of the new book, and still have no real ideas to work with. She obviously didn't get the hint when I changed my number.

I go to the fridge and get a beer. Better make it last, there's only three left and until my new bank card comes through there won't be any more. I look out of the dirty window into the shady alleyway below. Things are getting serious now: even when I get my bank card back, the account is almost empty, I've only done eleven hours for the language school this month, I owe a thousand euros in rent, and potentially now eight thousand quid of advance to pay back.

I once had a girlfriend back in Scotland, Lorna, who was into astrology, karma, healing crystals and all that shite. She always said the universe had a way of knowing when you needed something and providing for you. In my experience, what it generally provides is a kick in the bollocks.

CHAPTER TWO

I DON'T REMEMBER HOW I GOT TO KNOW IGNACIO. HE'S NOT ONE OF the artistic set, he certainly isn't a student, and as far as I can see he has no visible means of support. I suppose he's five years older than me, and handsome with that distinctively Spanish leanness born of chain-smoking and black coffee. He has a seemingly endless supply of women on his arm—these, too, always Olympic-standard smokers—and a bottomless fund of charm and anecdotes. We hit it off from the start: my Catalan was non-existent at that point, his English little better but we got by in Spanish. And for now, at least, I can trust him to stand me a night's drinks when he hears about my misfortune.

I dated his histrionic cousin Carmen for a couple of months. In the end I got fed up with kissing someone who tasted like an old ashtray and I wondered whether Ignacio would exact some kind of grotesque revenge when I ditched her. In fact he hardly seemed to notice, and Carmen herself took it with a kind of bored indifference.

We meet, as usual, in Periquito, a shit and sawdust old bar in scruffy Raval. It's themed around the Espanyol football team, with blue and white striped shirts all over the wall, although it's definitely taken to excess. "*Periquito*" is a budgerigar, the team's emblem, and the back of the bar is screened off into a makeshift wire enclosure, behind which a dozen or so budgies flitter, screech and shit. I assume the bar hasn't had a health and safety inspection in a while. As a kid, I grew up in the Moffat Stand watching Kilmarnock FC with my dad, back when he still used to leave the house. So I don't mind the footballing ambience, but I hate the little flying fuckers.

Luckily, I rarely have to get too close, because regardless of how cold it is, Ignacio will always want to sit outside so that he can smoke. Tonight is no different, except that when he turns up twenty minutes late, he has a woman by his side. This is not unusual, but the lassie is not his usual type, other than the fags. It's hard to tell as night falls on the ill-lit pavement, but she's probably forty-five, for a start. And she's British, which isn't his style at all.

"Tommy! Meet Hannah!" he says with a grin, signalling for three beers. "You will be friends; you are both English!"

"I'm Scottish," I growl. Catalans ought to get the difference, I think, but Ignacio never does.

Ignacio then sees someone he knows, which since he seems to know everyone is not surprising and slinks off to enjoy handshakes and some chaff about Espanyol's chances of beating Barcelona at the weekend.

The beers arrive, and Hannah sips from hers as she checks me over. She looks like she's come straight from work: a charcoal-grey trouser suit, a white blouse which probably had more buttons done up in the office. Her dark hair is pinned up on her head, and if not for her startling blue eyes, she could easily pass for a local. She has a raincoat draped over one seat, and if she's cold she doesn't show it.

"So you're a writer?" Her voice is low and well-modulated, sounds like it came from a private school somewhere down south. We might both be British, but we're not from the same place at all.

I shrug. "Of a sort."

She leans back. "Then I have a question."

I take a long slug of my beer. "'Where do you get your ideas?'"

She chuckles. "I don't know and I don't care. No, I wondered how you make a living from it."

I put my glass down. "You're very direct."

She runs a finger round the rim of her glass. "I can be. You don't have to tell me, of course."

"It's no secret. Most writers make almost no money, and I'm one of them. I teach English to young adults in the Barri Gòtic to pay the bills."

"Ignacio said so. Sunshine, a wonderful city, a nice job."

There's a hint of needle in her tone. I can't work out if it's bitchy or flirtatious.

"Let me tell you, it beats Kilmarnock in every way. What do you do?"

"*Advocat*. I run my own practice catering mainly to expats."

"A lawyer?" I catch myself smiling. "And you're snarking me for being a writer?"

She laughs. "I get by. Sometimes I meet interesting people." She looks straight into my face. I hold her gaze.

"How do you know Ignacio?" I say. He's still engrossed in football banter a few tables away.

"He does some odd jobs for me. As an expat, I find his contacts come in handy sometimes."

I try raising an eyebrow, which rarely works well. "You're not...?"

Her hand goes to a blouse button. "Ignacio? Please!"

"Sorry," I say. "But you came into the bar with him, and knowing Ignacio I thought..."

"I came to see you...Tommy."

This is an increasingly odd conversation, and I still can't work out what she wants, beyond the obvious—if that. I'm not exactly intrigued but I'm ready to hear more.

"I can't imagine you've read *Fear and Loathing in Kilmarnock*," I say, "so I don't know what Ignacio has said to you."

She lights another cigarette. "He told me he had an English friend who was a writer—"

"—I'm not—"

"—maybe a little down on his luck, charming, personable." She blows a plume of smoke into the air.

"None of those things is actively false, other than the nationality."

She reaches into her handbag. With a smile she pushes a business card across the table at me. "If you're interested in earning twenty thousand euros for three or four months' fairly easy work, come to my office at nine a.m. tomorrow. I need someone who's presentable, knows something about the arts, and can hold a conversation with a woman without looking at his shoes."

"Is tomorrow an interview?"

"We've just had it. You passed."

She stands up. "*Adéu*, Ignacio!" She waves to him and before I could say anything she's gone. On the bar sign above me, a budgie in an Espanyol shirt looks down on me with an unreadable expression.

CHAPTER THREE

It goes without saying that I'm going to turn up the next morning. A conversation commits me to nothing, and I could do with twenty grand. Coupled with my salary from the school, it might stave off returning to Kilmarnock for maybe two years. An upfront instalment would even cover my rent arrears.

Before I set off, I drop Polly a quick email to confirm my address—it's not like I'm important enough to warrant her turning up here. I also tell her that progress on the new book is slower than I'd hoped—strictly speaking, not a lie—and that I intend to have something for her to look at soon.

Hannah's office on Carrer de Balmes is only a couple of kilometres from my flat, so I don't bother trying to dodge the metro fare and walk through the drizzle instead. A brass plate on the wall next to a grubby Foto Express notes: *Sra. H. LAYTON, Advocat* with an arrow to the stairway.

At the top of the stairs a bored receptionist scrolls through Facebook. I give my name and without looking up, she waves me through the only other door.

Hannah sits at her desk, crisp and tidy in a navy suit.

"Tommy! *Bon dia!* Thank you for being punctual. Has Laura offered you drink?"

She comes round from behind her desk and we sit at a low pine coffee table in two easy chairs reclined almost horizontal.

"Drink?" I laugh. "Wee bitch didn't even offer a hello."

Hannah makes a 'what can you do?' gesture. "She's agency. Keeping staff in Barcelona is a nightmare."

She pokes her head out of the door, barks at Laura in Catalan. Laura's response is inaudible.

"I hope that's not the job you're offering me," I say. "I'm happy teaching English."

Hannah crosses her legs. "Fortunately not," she says briskly. "Before we start, I need you understand two things."

"I'm listening."

"One: everything we say here is confidential. Two: one of the reasons clients retain an *advocat* is to stay on the right side of the law. That means that occasionally they are straying close to the line. I am not asking you to break the law, but my clients are no angels."

Laura huffs in with two café solos, which she dumps with little ceremony on the table.

"*Gràcies,*" I say.

"Don't worry. She doesn't speak English. Now, are you happy with those conditions?"

"Sure."

"Good." She allows herself a crisp smile. "I doubt you are familiar with Club Artístic i Social d'Eixample."

I shake my head.

"It's a local social club interested in visual and written arts. They meet at a municipal building, the Galeria Artesana on Consell. It's not my scene, but I understand they're nice people if you like that kind of thing."

I wonder what Hannah's scene is, but this isn't the time

to ask.

"They have maybe a dozen members, but they're always on the lookout for more. In fact, they have an open event tomorrow."

Outside I can hear the traffic beginning to build. The window is shut to keep the fumes out, but the aircon gives a cool reassuring hum.

"You should go," says Hannah. "You like the arts, and they will be fascinated to meet a real writer. You might make some new friends."

"I don't need any new friends."

Hannah's smile doesn't reach the eyes. "Do the friends you have pay you twenty thousand euros?"

"You haven't mentioned anything which would warrant any payment."

"In business, contacts are everything. And this is a little clique that Ignacio can't help me with."

I sit up as straight as my seat will allow. "You'll need to be clearer about what you're expecting, especially if it's shady."

She sips her coffee. "Are you overburdened with scruples, Tommy? Are you so attached to them that you would rather live in Kilmarnock than Barcelona?"

"It's hard to give a hypothetical answer," I say, twisting my cup in my hand. "I won't pretend I'm any nobler than the next man. But I'm not going to kill anyone, or...I don't know."

"Tommy!" Her teeth when she smiles are sharp and white. "I've already said it's nothing illegal! The last time I looked, murder certainly was. Make a new friend—a lady friend—flirt with her a bit, maybe break her heart later on. Well, it happens. All's fair in love."

"I have no idea where this is going."

"You know how to flirt, don't you?" she says.

"You just put your lips together and blow. Or is that

whistling?"

She calls out into the reception to demand two more coffees.

"I don't know how into Catalan art you are," she says.

"Frankly, negligible. I hope that's not a deal-breaker."

"It's irrelevant," she says. "Picasso is the big name among painters here, of course. Miró, Dalí. Nothing like that in the Galeria Artesana, it's much too small, but sometimes they borrow minor pieces from the bigger museums. Have you ever been to the MACBA?"

"The modern art place in the Raval? Not really me. I might have gone once when I moved here and was doing the tourist thing."

"They have an interesting collection of Llorenç Llussà Moncada."

"Never heard of him. Not sure he was ever big in Kilmarnock."

"He was popular in the fifties and sixties, out here anyway. Surrealist, heavily influenced by Dalí. Forgotten for forty years, now highly collectable. Look him up online when you get home."

She reaches for a cigarette, offers me one which I decline, and lights up.

"Thanks for the tip, but I'm not in the business of art investment."

"Many people are," she says. "A rich man's game, at the top end. The last time a Llussà went to auction, it sold for $750,000."

"I'll make sure to start saving."

"I have a client," she says, leaning back, "who would love to expand his own collection. Unfortunately, they don't come on the market very often."

"I'm only peripherally interested in millionaires' frustrations."

"Tommy." She shakes her head. "Don't give me that chippy Scottish working class schtick."

I'm still not completely clear that she's not a bored cougar who fancies a bit of rough—which would explain Ignacio.

"My client," she says, "would be interested in acquiring pieces even where the provenance was not wholly—unblemished."

"And?"

"The director at MACBA is friends with the chairman of the governors at the Galeria Artesana. As a favour, he's letting the Galeria run a two-week exhibition on Llussà Moncada in August. The city's dead then, MACBA's not that busy, so he's lending out the Llussà collection to his friend. Charming."

"And?"

"The Galeria Artesana is a poky little place. The security is nothing compared to MACBA, where you can't fart without setting off an alarm."

"So your client wants to whip the Llussàs out of the Galeria Artesana..."

Hannah stubs out her cigarette.

"Let's say hypothetically."

"I thought I was on the hook for nothing illegal. I'd say art theft is pretty fucking criminal."

She shakes her head ruefully. "You'll note the word 'hypothetically'. That's why I'm a lawyer and I can afford to live in Sant Cugat."

Laura comes in with more coffee and attitude. I wait for her to slink back out.

"You want me to steal a painting? Are you mad?"

This time the smile flashes in her eyes. "Even by my standards, that would stretch hypothetical. Your job is much less risky, much more deniable."

I reach for the coffee, although God knows I'm jumpy enough already. "Go on."

"Your job is to get—my client—into the building."

"Getting hold of a key is worth twenty thousand euros?"

"It's a bit more complicated than that. There's an alarm system, access codes, maybe pressure plates and proximity detectors. They might not be up to MACBA standards, but they're not trivial. There's a lot of information, and a lot of toys, to neutralise the alarms."

"Why don't they just blow the bloody doors off?" I grin.

"This isn't the Italian Job," she says with a frown. "And maybe the less you know, the better. Just make a friend in the social club, tease the information out of her."

I'm not convinced of the approach's plausibility, but I am convinced by the cash. "Why not the Galeria staff?"

"The security on the Galeria side, including the staff, is reasonably tight. But nobody seems to have twigged that the social club meets in the same building."

She pushes a list across the table. "According to my records, which you can rely on, these people have both a key and the alarm codes. Any one of them can get in, not just to the building, but the gallery as well."

"You want me to honey-trap one of the women?"

"Well, a couple of them are men, but if they're arty types they're probably gay. The choice is yours if you want to swing that way."

"That's the plan? Surely there's an easier way."

"My client has considered a number of options," she says in a brassy voice. "He is paying, and this is how he wants to do it."

I steeple my fingers like a Bond villain. "How long do I have to do this?"

"Barcelona is almost empty in August, and that's when the

exhibition's on. We need to be ready by then. That's when it happens. Plenty of time."

"How many paintings are we talking about?"

"You don't need to know that."

"I'm just thinking—if one sells for three-quarters of a million dollars, and your client is helping himself to several, twenty thousand euros doesn't seem such a big cut."

Hannah laughs, perhaps the first genuine emotion I'd seen. "I warn you; the Russians are not people to chisel."

"'The Russians'?"

"That's what they call themselves. Who knows if they really are, but I wouldn't want to cross them."

"Negotiating my fee up front is neither chiselling nor crossing," I say. "Forty thousand, half up front."

She laughs again. "I wasn't sure how readily you'd take to the art world, but you'll fit right in. Twenty-five thousand, five thousand in hand, and only then because it's not my money."

Eventually we settle on thirty thousand, with the first ten in two advance instalments, plus out of pocket expenses.

"That's the deal," says Hannah. "But I warn you, don't try and take another bite later. The Russians are seriously dangerous people. Cross them, they'll fuck you up. If you do as you're told, you'll never meet them, and trust me, you don't want to."

I nod. The money seems pretty good for what I'm being asked to do. The women might be complete dogs for all I know, but they can't be as bad as all that, surely.

I stand up to leave.

"Now," she says. "Don't come here again. I'll text you when I want to meet."

"Don't you want my number, then?"

She smiles. "I already have it. *Adéu*, Tommy. Enjoy yourself at the open evening tomorrow."

CHAPTER FOUR

It's time to get ready for my first meeting with the suckers. I can't deny I'm excited. Thirty thousand euros is a life changing sum—for my life, anyway—but it's not that. Writers, even dormant ones, live inside their heads, and this is an adventure. Technically, it's a criminal conspiracy, but no-one's going to get hurt so I don't need to pretend I'm conscience-stricken about it.

I check my watch—I'll have to leave soon, so it's time to choose an outfit. I've already scoped out the bar we're meeting in. Broadway, an upmarket Art Deco bar spread over two floors on Carrer de Villaroel, just opposite the hospital. Handy for any alcohol-related accidents. Smart-casual is safest, but I wonder about a subtle rebellion by turning up in jeans and t-shirt: hey, look at me, I'm so arty I don't need to follow the rules. Or maybe go the other way, aim for a Raffles gentleman thief look and overdress. I don't really have the wardrobe for that, though.

In the end I settle on my only suit—navy blue, sharp creases because I haven't worn it since I've been out here—and a soft-collared pale blue shirt. No tie, I'm an artist, not an accountant. The trousers are a bit loose and I cinch the belt in a notch. I look in the full-length mirror: not bad. It would be better with shades but I'd look a twat turning up with them pushed back on my head on a February evening. I'll be fine without them. Does this scream distinguished foreign writer, hot and worth talking to? Close enough, or as close as I can manage anyway.

I nod at myself in the mirror and switch off the light before I lock the door. *Let's go to work.*

Broadway is as classy as I remember it. It's got a nice, relaxed vibe, but clean with it. No fucking budgies flying around in here. Winter evenings in Barcelona are cold, whatever you might imagine about the place, and I don't have an overcoat that doesn't make me look like a tourist or a student. With only a jacket and shirt against the chill, I'm glad to get inside.

The upper floor of Broadway, with a gallery looking out over the area below, isn't that busy, and I recognise the club members immediately from the photos on their Facebook page. They're clustered round the bar and there aren't that many of them. I can see why they might want new members: there are a couple of guys and maybe five or six girls. I've been emailing the 'social secretary', Estel about tonight and she looks up as I walk over and waves at me.

She takes me by the arm and leads me over to the bar. "I am so glad you could come," she says in Catalan. "We don't have any writers in our group."

"I'm not really—" I reply in the same language. "I dabble..."

She indicates her opinion of my Catalan by switching to fluent but heavily accented English. "Here, we are all artists," she says with a grin. "All as good as each other."

I look into her grey eyes and smile. She has a natural vivacity that I respond to immediately—that, and the figure her green dress sets off to advantage. Her dark blonde hair is held back off her face with a clip.

"So what do you do?" I ask, giving up on the Catalan.

"I'm an actress," she says. "Part-time, anyway. The rest of the time I work in accounts." Her expression suggests how much she enjoys that.

"I teach English as well as write," I say. "The language school in Barri Gòtic."

"Ah yes! A good way to meet people."

"Teenagers," I smile. "They are good kids, but... you know."

A tall slender figure slides up beside her and puts a hand on her forearm. "So, who have you got here?"

Estel gives a brisk smile. "Jaume, this is Tommy. He is an English writer—" I let this slide "—and Tommy, meet Jaume."

I shake hands in what I hope is a bluff hearty fashion. "Pleased to meet you. You are an artist?"

He looks down his nose. "An artist of the human condition, you might say."

Or I might not. I have absolutely no idea what this means and I doubt that Jaume does either. I'm here as a bullshitter, and I recognise another one in front of me.

"Jaume *observes*," says Estel. "And then he sometimes shares his observations. His canvas is humanity."

Jaume's eyes narrow. There's history between these two. I'll need to understand the dynamics of this group, particularly if I'm going to seduce Estel.

Estel is keen to find someone else to introduce me to, and I'm hardly sorry to leave Jaume behind. She beckons one of the other guys, who's introduced as Aleix. He's a painter and enthusiastic about his art. He has on black skin-tight shirt and trousers, a diamond earring and matching pendant at his open neck. I feel justified in concluding that he's gay, and I warm to him because that suggests he's not going to seduce anyone who interests me. I need not consider him a threat or a rival. I'm going to have to pick someone to try and seduce and, based on first impressions it's probably going to be Estel.

The group is, in fact, almost exclusively female. Montse is older than the rest, earnest but likeable. Then Salut and Mèlia: two slim birdlike brunettes, one a sculptor and the other a dancer. The last one I'm introduced to is Beatriz, a girl maybe a couple of years younger than me, medium height, slender almost to boyishness, with coppery hair in a scruffy ponytail. Her sharp nose hangs above a pensive mouth, and her only striking feature is her enormous and expressive brown eyes. She's pretty, in a girl next door sort of way, but you wouldn't lie awake at night thinking about her.

Everyone else is clotted in their own little groups, and I find myself alone with Beatriz. Our conversation doesn't really get beyond small talk. I find out that she's an artist—although not what sort—and works as a graphic designer. She's cagey about where she lives— "over that way", with a loose flap of her arm—and doesn't seem that disposed for conversation. She doesn't seem that taken with me, and if I was following my own inclination, I'd probably have chatted up one of the others, but I feel an obligation to charm where I can tonight.

"I teach at the English language school," I say. "Yours is excellent." This is true—idiomatic with a good accent. She makes a little noise— *"foof!"*—and shakes her head. With an approach to a smile, she says: "I thought so, but I can't always follow you. Your accent is unusual."

I laugh. "That's because I'm Scottish. Sometimes even the English can't understand me. I'm from somewhere called Kilmarnock."

"Kil-mar-nock? I don't know that word. Is it a nice place?"

"No. Not at all. I like Barcelona much better."

She ponders this for a moment. "It is sad that you don't like your home."

"You get more sunshine in a week here than we get in a year in Scotland. And I like the people too." I practice a smile.

She looks at me with those eyes again. I don't know if she doesn't have a sense of humour, just doesn't find me charming, or maybe she's nervous. Before she can reply, Aleix appears to make his farewells. Seeing his clothes, I might have got away with dressing up a bit more. I don't know whether they're expensively tailored or just well-chosen.

"*Bona nit,*" he says. "Tomàs, a pleasure to meet you!"

Beatriz laughs and kisses him on both cheeks. "*Bona nit,* Aleix."

Jaume, meanwhile, takes his leave of us with a frosty nod. A good job that Hannah did not want me to seduce him. Next to me, I sense Beatriz stiffen. Is there anybody who doesn't hate the little shite? Perhaps the easiest way to get the information is just to beat it out of him, then I don't need to worry about a seduction with all its potential pitfalls. But the last time I hit someone I was thirteen and it hadn't ended well.

Estel comes over and throws her arms around Beatriz. "Shall we share a taxi, Triz? I can't face the metro."

Beatriz nods and puts her bag over her shoulder. Estel leans in and gives me a double-kiss. "It was so nice to meet you, Tommy. You must come again and read from your work."

"Only if you want me to bore everyone to death. I don't think your group would be too interested in dreary Scottish life."

"Perhaps," says Beatriz, "we would enjoy hearing about Kil-mar-nock." Is there a flicker of a smile behind her eyes?

And with that they are all gone. I know I'll be seeing them again soon.

CHAPTER
FIVE

It's gone two a.m. by the time I get back to Baixada del Silur but I don't feel sleepy. What my flat gains in affordability it loses in comfort, and this extends to the bed. I pour myself a glass of wine and put the cork back in the bottle.

I open the window and look out over the alley, which at this time of night is deserted. The evening, as far as it goes, has been a good start. I've made one enemy, but this is a plus. The strutting hipster obviously enjoys being the alpha male, and the fact that he doesn't like me probably makes the others look on me more favourably.

If I was looking for someone to date, I'm sure I'd choose Estel, who can carry her end of a conversation and most of mine too. She's friendly, open and I can't deny that I wouldn't mind seeing what she looks like with no make-up first thing in the morning.

But I'm not following my own inclinations. I'm doing a job, distasteful as it might be. And so I allow myself to think of women beyond Estel. (Out of completeness I also consider Aleix, who's clearly gay. While I wouldn't describe myself as homophobic, my first foray into art theft probably doesn't need to be accompanied by this particular experiment). Montse is too old—sorry, I'm sure you're lovely! —and not being able to tell Salut and Mèlia apart doesn't augur well there either. So the only other woman I've got beyond exchanging names with is Beatriz.

And Beatriz, in this context, is immediately perfect. She'd seemed shy but not obviously sociopathic, and she's in Estel's shadow. Surely she'd welcome some attention?

I have most of tomorrow free—I'm not teaching a class until five o'clock—and after getting to sleep at about four a.m. I doze until some clown outside with a boom-box wakes me at nine. My iPhone—probably an unwise extravagance—has a text from an unknown number but it's not difficult to guess who it's from:

meet me at the joan miro foundation montjuic 1pm for debrief + first instalment of fee.

I could really have done without seeing Hannah today but there's no way of getting the cash without it. The timing gives me ample time for lunch afterwards without being late for my class.

There's nothing in the fridge for breakfast so, after showering, I check my phone is fully charged and skip down the steep flight of stairs and out on to Baixada del Silur. The narrow alley hasn't yet caught the sun and although it's ten o'clock I'm shivering in the sharp breeze. Omar's, my favourite local café, is busy, so I step into the less prepossessing one on Carrer de

Rabassa. This has the virtue of being almost empty, so I pick up a discarded copy of *Sport* while I wait for my almond croissant and coffee. The paper, as ever, concentrates on the exploits of FC Barcelona rather than their smaller city rivals Espanyol, whose results I follow in a desultory way after going to a few matches with the tickets Ignacio has scrounged. *Amunt les periquits!* Up the budgies!

It will only take me three-quarters of an hour to get the metro and funicular to Montjuïc, so I drink a couple more coffees before taking myself to the rendezvous.

For reasons I've never understood, riding the funicular always puts me in a good mood. Today, outside the main tourist season, it's hardly busy and I sit back to enjoy the crawl up the steep slope and the views out over the city.

The Miró museum is easy enough to find, being almost next to the funicular exit. I'd spent a lot of time in the gardens of Montjuïc as a pseudo-tourist during my first months in Barcelona, enjoying the presence of a dwarf mountain in one of the biggest cities in Europe.

I'm five minutes early, and there's no sign of Hannah. Even as I look, though, she emerges from a wooded path leading up to the building, where no doubt she's been waiting in concealment. She has on a pair of shapeless cargo pants, a blue fleece with "I Heart Barcelona", a bum-bag and a white baseball cap.

"You haven't come from the office, then," I say.

"It's as well to be discreet. Let's go and sit on the bench and pretend to be tourists."

I'm not sure I'm attired for that—my look is more louche university professor, which I suppose isn't so far from the truth.

We both lean forward on the bench. There's a chilly wind and I hope we won't be here too long.

She pulls a packet of cigarettes out from her fleece pocket before putting them back. "I'm never sure if you're allowed to smoke out here," she says. "It was much easier before the smoking ban."

"Not one of my vices," I say with a bleak smile.

"You have enough others, I'm sure. Now, tell me about last night."

"Money first."

She raises an eyebrow. "Well, I have fostered a little mercenary, haven't I?"

"I'm not doing this for shits and giggles, Hannah," I say with a hint of tetchiness. "Either pay me or piss off."

This time she laughs. "I'm your employer now, so 'Senyora Layton' might be more appropriate. But the fish always fights the hook."

I wonder if there had ever been a Senyor Layton. If so, I imagine he's long dead, his bones lying picked clean and white in the mountains to the north.

I hold out my hand. "Money, Senyora Layton, *si us plau.*"

"There, a little a politeness never hurt anyone, did it? And your Catalan is improving. My headmistress at Cheltenham always used to say please and thank-you were the most important words in life." She reaches into her bum-bag and pulls out an envelope sealed tight with parcel tape. "That's the first five thousand. You'll get the rest of the advance next time."

This isn't ideal, but I'm five thousand euros richer than I'd been this morning so I decide not to push it further. I can at least pay my rent off before it becomes a bigger problem.

I run her briefly through the previous night's events.

"Promising enough start," she says. She pulls out her cigarettes again and lights one. "Fuck it. What's the worst that can happen?"

"Lung cancer. Heart disease. Emphysema."

"Christ, Chisholm, you're a fucking ray of sunshine. I hope you're a bit more cheerful with the Spanish girls."

"Don't worry. They seemed to like me enough last night."

This isn't strictly true, I admit. Estel is naturally friendly and the others hadn't been that bothered one way or the other. I'd probably got on best with Aleix but I decide not to go there.

"So, have you picked a victim?"

I wince and scratch the stubble on my chin. "Humour me and don't rub in that this is a callous con trick."

"It doesn't do to get sentimental. One of these girls is going to give you the key and the door codes, and any other security measures we'll need to disable to get some paintings out. Get used to it."

"What if I tricked it out of someone else? Jaume didn't seem very bright."

Hannah takes a long drag on her cigarette. "Look, you do you, Chisholm. But the Russians want results, and that means so do I. Tell me there's a better way to do this and I'll consider it. But there's not."

"So she's lying there gasping in an orgasmic flush and my pillow talk is 'what's the access code, darling?'"

"I'm quivering just thinking about it, Chisholm."

I stand up.

"You don't like it," she says, "give me the money back, then you can starve or fuck off back to Kilmarnock."

"I didn't say that." I sit back down. "My concerns are practical, not moral."

"I'm glad to hear it. You're making it more difficult than it needs to be. Take your time—within reason—and it will all come together."

I stand up again.

"Wait here for five minutes," she says, "and then walk back

through the trees. I'll text you about another meeting. And the rest of the money."

I slump back on the bench. "*Adéu*, Senyora Layton," I hiss at her retreating back.

I'm probably not at my best with the evening class that night. I still haven't calmed down from meeting Hannah, even though I have an envelope with five grand in my pocket. Her mixture of callousness and deliberate superiority is grit in my eye, and not for the first time I wonder if she is an ideal associate. But then again, I also wonder how much I want to go back to Kilmarnock, and that's its own answer. And I can't deny a certain relish at the thought of starring in my own heist movie. Art theft is a victimless crime so I might as well enjoy what is certain to be a once in a lifetime experience.

PART TWO

17-18 MARCH 2014

CRUSH (AND NAIVETY)

I

Ironically, when I finally do click with Beatriz, it's nothing to do with manipulation or seduction strategies. If there's a lesson in that, I don't learn it.

The club holds occasional evening exhibitions of its members' work which are open to the public. I'm particularly excited by this, not because I'm especially ardent to see Salut's sculptures, but for the chance to visit the Artesana for the first time. Here at last I will see the keypads and other security measures that I'm going to help Hannah's Russians break.

I get there about eight-thirty after my class. The door to the foyer is already open so I don't get to see the locks in action, but I note a keypad, itself protected by a locked glass cabinet. I'll need not only the code but keys to the outer door and the glass cabinet.

Three doors lead off the foyer. In the centre is the auditorium used by local theatrical groups; to the left is the entrance to the main gallery—where presumably the Llorenç Llussà Moncada collection will hang in August—while the right gives onto a smaller space which tonight has been purposed for our exhibition.

Jaume patrols the entrance, favouring me with a haughty glance. I'm used to his frostiness by now, and clearly he's only hanging around the doorway because he doesn't have anything to exhibit: the 'art of the human condition' does not readily lend itself to installations. Estel had told me he'd once had an actual art exhibition, which had been shut down by the local health and safety inspectorate, before it had even opened. I didn't know whether to believe this was true, or even possible.

I get inside and all the old gang are there. Mèlia hands me a glass of rioja which I sip as I take in the various items. There are a few faces I don't recognise, presumably members of the public or friends of the artists, or even vagrants who have wandered in off the street.

Estel and Beatriz are talking in one of the corners, but the nearest installation is Montse's, a series of interactive models representing scenes from the Spanish Civil War. Tonight she has on severe glasses and a beret. The models are interesting and informative, although no-one else seems fussed, and we have a brief conversation about Orwell's *Homage to Catalonia* which appears to improve her opinion of me.

Aleix is standing proudly by half a dozen of his paintings and shakes my hand with a grin. Perhaps reflecting my lack of imagination, I expected his work to be bold, vivid and flamboyant. In fact, the paintings are a series of pleasant but unremarkable watercolours depicting the city's landmarks. They remind me more than anything of Hitler's watercolours in his days of Viennese poverty before he took up dictatorship and genocide. Even though I judge the risk of Aleix following a similar path is low, I keep my thoughts to myself.

Estel appears at my shoulder with a trill. "Tomàs!" She grabs my elbow. "I have made an exhibition for you!"

Glad to be free of the responsibility of praising Aleix's paintings any further, I follow her to the back of the room, to find a poster-sized version of my author picture from *Fear and Loathing in Kilmarnock*, alongside two or three copies of the book. I hadn't realised it was even available in Spain, but such is the inescapable reach of Amazon, I suppose. She's even printed out my review from the *Guardian*. Luckily, the *Scotsman* piece, which had described my depiction of Kilmarnock as "insulting, patronising and grossly offensive", has eluded her research.

"Thank you," I say, genuinely touched that she's gone to such trouble to make me feel included. I like her much better than Hannah Layton and I wonder—shamefully, for the first time—what will happen to the club once it becomes known that their access codes have been used to rob the Artesana. Maybe I had been too quick to dismiss this as a victimless crime.

"I love your picture," she says. "Cheekbones!"

I've always liked the photo too. It's excessively flattering, a reflection not of my cheekbones but the exceptional skill of the photographer's lighting technician.

"Where did you find all this?"

"You can do anything on the internet," she says with a dimple.

Jaume manifests at our side. He is most unwilling to allow me unfettered conversation with any of the women, which is perhaps why I usually end up spending so much time talking to Aleix.

"Do you perhaps, Tommy," says Jaume, "have another novel coming out soon? If so I will have to read this one quickly to be ready for it."

"You're all right, pal," I say. "We're a little way from the next one."

"Ah!" He throws up a hand. "I am sure, of course, that it will be worth the wait. How wonderful it must be, to be truly talented and successful! Don't you think so, Estel?"

"I wouldn't know, Jaume, and neither would you." There's colour in her cheeks. "And I am sure Tomàs is too modest to describe himself that way."

There's a seething dislike here, on both sides. I'm keen to find Beatriz, although I can't see where she is, but I feel some obligation to support Estel in her unfathomable battle.

Luckily, as so often, Aleix appears. Jaume notably simmers down, for Aleix is no threat to his dominion over the ladies. Estel too relaxes. It's too late now to wonder if pretending to be gay would have been my best course. In the dynamics of the group, Aleix is the only one everyone trusts.

Leaving him to hold the fort, I resume my circuit of the exhibition. Salut has created some small bronze sculptures that are probably best described as 'abstract' and after a few anodyne remarks I move on before Jaume arrives to chase me off here too.

And here, at last, is Beatriz, looking thoughtfully at a series of collages. These are the first objects that I've seen that I actually like. They consist of everyday objects photographed from unusual angles, augmented and extended by ink drawings in some cases, with parts of other images cut out, and juxtaposed in startling and sometimes alarming ways. A couple of them have fabrics attached, and the overall effect is striking in a way I can't define.

I smile at Beatriz. "These are the best things here," I say. "Aren't they wonderful?"

"You like them?"

She has on a teal sleeveless blouse to reveal an intricate swirling tattoo covering the entirety of her upper left arm. Her hair is pinned up on one side. A brown suede miniskirt with a superfluity of buckles sits above black tights.

"Don't you?" I say. "I shouldn't say it, but these are the only things here that I would buy." I'm struck by a thought. "Although of course I haven't seen yours yet, and I'm sure they are beautiful too." *Lucky escape there.*

She smiles and her eyes light up. Suddenly I wonder how I could ever have found her ordinary.

"These are mine," she says. Her cheek is slightly flushed.

"Well, I didn't know," I laugh. "So you can tell I meant it and I wasn't just flattering you."

Her eyes narrow. "You don't think I could do this work? That it's just a hobby like—" She breaks off but her eyes involuntarily slide towards Aleix's stand.

She's prickly, but I've found something she's passionate about.

"These are incredible pieces of work, Beatriz," I say. "That's all I mean. I really admire them, and so that must mean I admire the artist."

She says nothing for a moment. I've never known anyone who can pause a conversation like her, turn things over in her mind before she decides where to go.

"Thank you. You know what it is like, to put something of yourself—of your heart—into the world for other people to touch and mock and spoil. It is the hardest part, much harder than making the thing, no?"

I'd always enjoyed showing off my work and how clever it made me look, and by the time I was twelve I knew writing was my way out of Kilmarnock. But I understand what she means anyway.

"Of course," I say. "But then when someone gets what you're trying to do, it's all worth it, isn't it?"

She pauses again. She touches my elbow almost too fleetingly to notice. "Yes. Yes it is."

"When the exhibition is finished," I say, my gulp surely audible, "would you like to get dinner?"

I doubt practised seducers feel like they're fourteen years old, but you work with what you've got.

"Of course. We are all going anyway to Broadway. I thought you knew."

"That wasn't quite what I meant. Perhaps tomorrow, the two of us..."

Once again the pause, the deep reflection packed into a quarter of a second. Whoever said the Spanish were impulsive and mercurial had never met Beatriz Bernat.

"I don't think that is a good idea," she says. "I am not very good at... and the last time I... well, I don't think it would end happily."

"How do you know?" This isn't about Hannah's scheme now. It's not even about fragile male vanity—or not much.

She shrugs. "I don't like risks. And I hardly know you—not well enough to trust you."

Ludicrously, given that making this work is worth thirty thousand euros to me, I don't want to push her. There is a vulnerability just below the surface that I can sense and don't want to disturb.

"I'm sorry," I say. "I didn't mean to unsettle you. And I really do like the collages, I wasn't just saying that."

She smiles again, more relaxed and maybe relieved. "I will sell them when I have a few more," she says. "Maybe fifty euros each. But choose one, to keep. My gift."

I look away before I can stop myself. I'm touched, because we both know how much these pieces mean to her.

"Have I said something wrong?" Her eyebrows knit together in concern.

"No," I say. "You've done nothing wrong at all, Beatriz. And if you're serious, the one with the cat is just beautiful."

She beams. "Once we pack the exhibition up, it's yours."

As I smile, she rips a strip off the red paper tablecloth the exhibits are standing on. "Write down your number on that," she says, making to walk off. "Perhaps I'll text you."

And with that she's gone. I have to admire the poise: no opportunity for me to respond, no giving me her number. All the control is hers.

I realise that thirty thousand euros or not, Beatriz is someone I would very much want to get to know anyway.

2

HANNAH SUMMONS ME TO CAFÈ VIENA, AN AIRY AND SPACIOUS BAR ON Carrer de Ferran in the old Barri Gòtic. Given her preference to pass as a tourist for our assignations, I'm surprised she hasn't chosen the Starbucks next door.

The Viena is far less busy though and that makes it easier for her to pass me the envelope with the second five thousand euros.

"I'm hoping," she says, "that you have some progress to report by now."

I sit back and take a pull at my coffee. "I've got to know them all now. Some—candidates—are more promising than others."

Her hands play with her lighter, the packet of cigarettes sitting untouched on the table in front of her.

"We're getting beyond the time for reconnaissance now, Chisholm. Less talk, more action."

"It's not as easy as you think."

"If it was easy, I'd get Ignacio to do it for five thousand euros and pocket the difference. It's decision time, sunshine. Who have you chosen, and what's the plan?"

I think for a moment. I don't want to be too open, but I don't have much choice.

"Beatriz Bernat."

"I didn't hear you."

"Fuck you, senyora. You're not deaf."

She leans forward. "Fuck *you,* Chisholm. You don't realise how very antisocial the Russians can be. So I need something I can give to them."

"Don't pass on names."

A half-smile twitches her lips. "And why not? You don't want to get her into trouble?"

"Not exactly."

"Understand this, Chisholm. You *are* in trouble. We need to stamp on scruples and sentimentality right now. Beatriz Bernat is a tool, no more and no less than the alarm codes."

I slam my cup down. "I didn't think you heard her name."

"I memorised the keyholder list," she says.

"So...do you know any of these people? Have you met them?"

I'm interested, in spite of myself, in what she'd made of Beatriz. But Hannah shakes her head.

"Never seen them, never want to. Your job is to manage them, my job is to manage you. I don't know which of us is the bigger sucker."

"I imagine your cut is more than thirty thousand euros, which answers that question."

Hannah puts the lighter down. "We've discussed this. Your fee is fixed, and if you try and fuck about with that now, you'll be found floating face down in the Port de Barcelona."

I sigh. "I'm not dissatisfied with the fee."

"You're pissed off about something."

I measure my words carefully. "I didn't expect to feel sorry for—for any of them."

Hannah gives a thin-lipped smile. "You've taken the money, and now you want to ease your conscience by pretending you feel bad about it. If that makes you happier, fine, but I'd advise you to get a fucking grip."

The only fucking grip I want to take just then is around her throat. She can see it, and it seems to amuse her.

"You have empathy," she says with a cool inspection of my face. "I could never see the use for it myself, but for what you're being asked to do, I suppose it will come in helpful. Just make it, you know, one-way empathy: get her to like you. You don't have to like her back."

"One-way empathy is not empathy at all."

She stands up, signals for the bill. "Next time I see you, have something concrete to report." And then she's gone, leaving me to pick up the tab.

I call Ignacio, whom I haven't seen for a while, and we meet at Periquito. An advertising board depicting two glum budgerigars makes a wan attempt to attract patrons.

Tonight he has no women on his arm, and greedily attacks the tapas I've paid for. We're indoors and I can see the tweeting birds flittering behind their wire screen.

"How well do you know Hannah Layton?" I ask.

Ignacio wipes his fingers with unexpected daintiness. "I do a few jobs for her. I wouldn't say we're friends."

"Jobs?"

"Why do you want to know? Run a few packages here, pick a guy up from the airport there, maybe book a hotel."

"Is it all legit?"

"Come on, man! Sometimes it's best not to ask. That's my line and I'd suggest it's yours too."

I'm not completely reassured. Am I the only one signed up

to do something crooked for her, or is she completely bent? "So you think she's shady?"

"What is this, man? You like her or something?"

"Not exactly," I say carefully, draining my glass with a grim flourish.

"Hey! Not my type, but why not?"

"You don't make her sound trustworthy."

Ignacio shrugs. "Probably not. But you're not planning to marry her. Are you?"

I signal for two more beers.

"You know she wanted me to do some work for her?"

"Of course. I recommended you."

"That's my only interest in her. Can I trust her?"

Ignacio chases an olive around the bowl with a stick. "She'll pay you if she said she will."

"And how..."

"How what?"

"How deep is she? With things that would interest the police?"

Ignacio picks at his teeth with the stick. "She knows the law. I'd think she'd know what she can and can't do."

"That's not what I asked."

"Hey, Tommy! Lighten up. I don't know everything she does, and I don't care. She pays me cash for things that don't seem like trouble. If she's asked you to do more, that's between the two of you. And I don't want to know."

I sit back in the chair. "Have you ever heard the Russians mentioned?"

Ignacio snaps the cocktail stick with a brisk instinctive motion. "Yes. And I wish you hadn't. Watch your back, man, watch your back."

My phone beeps and I look down at the incoming text.

sorry about the other night. would love to go for a drink. Btz x

I push my glass away and throw down ten euros on the table. "*Gràcies*, Ignacio. Got to go."

I store Beatriz's number in my contacts and text her back.

Ready when u are where r u?

I always take a childish delight in using text-speak even though I know it makes me look like I'm twelve.

A couple of minutes later she responds.

Now?

Sure. Im in raval

I can see dots on the screen where she's typing. They disappear, and then come back.

That's near me. Do you know el gat blau on c/del carme

. . .

I don't but among the obstacles I'm facing this has to be most surmountable.

Ill find it

It turns out El Gat Blau—the blue cat, my Catalan is improving—is two minutes' walk away round the corner, so I'm there first. It's an arty little place, an eighties vibe, prints, posters and collages on the walls. There's a blue neon sign of a plump cat above the door, the bulbs in one of the ears flickering erratically. If I'd imagined a bar where Beatriz would choose to hang out, this is it.

I get a beer while I'm waiting and bag a table with rickety plastic seats near the door. Ten minutes later she's here. El Gat isn't a place you dress up for, and she certainly hasn't: faded ripped jeans, a sleeveless Stranglers t-shirt, scuffed blue plimsolls. She comes over, kisses me on the cheek, throws her leather jacket on a chair and sits down.

Catching the barman's eye she signals for a drink. "Hey Xabi!" she says. He smiles back. "*Hola Beatriz!*"

So she's a regular here.

She gives a soft little smile. "I forgot to give you the print," she says.

"That's OK. Whenever's convenient – if you still want to? It's too nice to give away."

She pushes her fringe out of her eyes. "No, it's yours. I can't sell them all, and you seemed to like it so much." Her eye catches mine and darts away again.

"I did. You're really talented." I'm conscious this is the lamest observation I could make.

She points at one of the prints on the wall. "That one's mine."

"You're doing better than me. I can't remember when I last sold anything." *Largely because I can't remember when I last wrote anything.*

She laughs. "I won't be giving up my job on sixty euros."

She pauses and sips at the beer which has arrived, the foam flecking her upper lip. She licks it off like a cat. "I'm sorry about last time," she says.

"You don't have to be, really," I say. "I'm sure you're not short of offers."

This seems to be the wrong thing to say, although I can't work out why. She retreats back into herself. Eventually she says, "I broke up with someone." She shrugs. "You can't see you're an idiot at the time. I don't want to make the same mistake again. So sometimes I can be—repulsive, is that a word?"

I can't help laughing. "It is, but I don't think it means what you think it does. You are very very far from repulsive."

"I push people away. Repel?"

"Yes, that's a word, but if you say something's repulsive in English it means disgusting."

She laughs too. It lights up her face. "Maybe I should join your class."

"You don't need it."

She's starting to relax. She orders mojitos, which come in jam-jars and last five minutes, then I get some more. We talk about her job, childhood as the middle girl, a sanitised take on life in Kilmarnock—Kil-mar-nock—all the things you cast about when you're getting to know someone. She is most animated on her art, and I wonder why I can't feel like that about my own writing. She's putting together pieces for an exhibition she hopes to get at a private gallery on the Carrer de Petritxol, which it seems would be a big deal. I notice that she's most alive and enthusiastic when she seems to forget I'm there. This is hardly flattering, but I'm fascinated by her: the mixture of passion and reserve, the startling openness when she overcomes her hesitation. I push aside thoughts of Hannah and access codes and settle into enjoying the evening with someone I would find enthralling whether I was being paid to or not.

Before we know it, it's one-thirty. She knocks back her last mojito and then eats the mint sprig from the jar with a giggle. I think she's a little drunk, finding reasons to touch my hand as we talk. She is certainly not being repulsive, not in any possible meaning of the word.

"Did you say you live near here?"

"Carrer del Tigre," she says. "It's only five minutes away."

The Raval has always struck me as a hip and lively neighbourhood, but also somewhere you might not want to be a woman out alone late at night.

"Can I walk you home?" I say.

She gives an odd little laugh. "A gentleman! Or not a gentleman at all."

I am baffled by the remark. She's rapidly declining in coherence, drunker than she looks.

"A man who walks you home is either being kind, or he wants to fuck you. Do you want to fuck me?"

I reflect that the fifth and sixth mojitos had probably not been a good idea. I scratch my chin. "Whatever I say would be an insult one way or another. I'm going to take you home and say *bona nit* and we'll talk tomorrow."

She ponders my response and seems to find it satisfactory. She tries to put both arms in the same sleeve of her jacket, which after a few moments of amusement I fix.

We stand up to go, and the barman Xabi comes over. "You OK, Beatriz?" he asks in Catalan. He probably thinks I've spiked her drinks. She puts a hand on his arm. "I think I'll have a headache tomorrow," she laughs.

Xabi eyes me suspiciously. "I haven't seen you in here before." He takes his phone out of his back pocket and quickly takes a picture of me. "I'm sure you're a nice guy, but just in case."

If a fella had done this to me in Kilmarnock he'd have been shitting teeth for a week and his phone would have been at the bottom of the River Irvine. But I was feeling unaccountably mellow and, although he was a pushy wee gobshite, I kind of admired him looking out for Beatriz. "Don't worry, pal," I say. "You'll see me again."

Even in Barcelona, the evenings are cool in March. Beatriz is shivering and leans against me. I can't tell if it's the cocktails, the cold, or...it hardly matters.

I don't know the way so Beatriz must be directing our steps, although I can't tell how she's doing it. Soon enough we're at Carrer del Tigre. The metal shutters of the shops are tagged with copious graffiti. In this, at least, it resembles Kilmarnock, although there the walls are defaced with poorly executed obscenity. In Barcelona, though, even the graffiti is art. The district is rough and ready, but it's not without charm.

"Why are you smiling?" She is literally hanging off me like I'm a lamppost.

I indicate the graffiti. "I thought you'd live somewhere classier."

"It's fun here," she says. "Lively. It's not as bad as it looks."

She fumbles in her bag for keys and at the third attempt unlocks the metal grille leading to her stairway.

"Are you sure you won't come up?" she says, now looking a bit more sober.

Hannah would have told me to go in, of course, for coffee or whatever else might follow. We might even get straight to access codes. But I can't think of any possible outcome which won't look much worse in the morning. If we both escape with just hangovers we've got off lightly.

I shake my head. "Thanks. But I've got an early start tomorrow."

"I've got your print upstairs."

I smile. "Give it to me tomorrow."

The concept of tomorrow briefly seems to challenge her. Then she kisses me on both cheeks. "*Bona nit,* Tomàs," she says. "And *gràcies.*" I don't know what she's got to thank me for.

"*Bona nit,* Beatriz."

I wait until she locks the door behind her and hear her skip erratically up the stairs. After a minute, as I turn to go, I see a lamp come on in the first floor window. She moves into the light to pull the shutter down and catches sight of me in the street below. She opens the door onto the tiny balcony and steps out, blowing me a kiss before retreating back inside.

I wait a few more minutes until the light goes out and stare up at the balcony. *Romeo and fucking Juliet. With mojitos and graffiti. And look how that turned out.*

Has the evening been a success? I'm too tired, buzzing from the mojitos, and Beatriz, to be able to tell. It will all make more sense tomorrow. The metro will long since have closed, so I set off for the hike back to Baixada del Silur.

PART THREE
19—20 MARCH 2014

STAR CHARMER

I

The next morning I wake late, sluggish and strung out. I've slept longer than I expected, but that's probably the mojitos. I certainly don't feel refreshed, and when I rub my hand over my stubble, the rasping sets off flares in my brain.

I pick up my phone to see if I have any messages. Blank. Is that good? It's a relief to have nothing from Hannah. There's no way I can give her a coherent debrief. Beatriz has work this morning so she might be up and about, but I'll text her later. I'm not sure how she'll feel about last night, or even how much she'll remember. She was beyond puggled.

My one remaining bottle of water in the fridge is almost empty, and the leftover food makes my stomach roil. I drink what water is left, clean my teeth and stand under the hottest shower I can bear for five minutes. I wouldn't say I'm a new man after, but I'm together enough to get dressed, get some coffee and an omelette in Omar's, and scrape together some supplies at the Consum supermarket on Escorial.

In the circumstances, the excursion is a triumph over adversity, and I crawl back to the apartment before the sun gets settled. It's not hot yet but the light's not helping my sore head.

My phone's still dormant, and I start to think about texting Beatriz. If this was a normal dating thing, I'd let her come to me, but I've got a job to do and I need to get back in touch. How will she have viewed last night? She's probably hungover, and perhaps embarrassed about the scene outside her flat. I'm guessing she doesn't normally get hammered on cocktails on a Tuesday night, particularly in a bar where people know her, and it wouldn't be that hard for her to blame me.

Still, if she wants an apology, no doubt she'll find a way of making that clear. In the end I ignore any downsides of the evening and simply send

gràcies – had a great time last night x

and leave it at that.

My hangover is getting worse, shower, fresh air and breakfast having failed to do the trick. With no classes today, I've got nothing on until meeting Ignacio to watch football this evening, so I go back to bed. By the time I wake in the late afternoon, I'm at least partly refreshed. I turn over to look at my phone, which glares back with an empty screen. Rolling out of bed for the second time that day, I have another shower and make myself a sandwich.

I meet Ignacio at Periquito. We'd get a better TV in one of the clinical sports bars in Poble Nou or Barceloneta, but when Espanyol are playing at home, this is the next best thing to being at the match. I feel overdressed in jeans with a linen shirt and jacket—pretty much everyone else, including Ignacio, is in an Espanyol shirt. The budgies in their cage share the excitement, or at least agitation, but the TV is turned up so loud that their chirping is drowned out.

The game is a scruffy 1-1 draw, and I miss Espanyol's goal trying to pre-empt the half-time rush for the one toilet. Ignacio, unusually for him, is pensive and uncommunicative, which I put down to Espanyol's uninspiring performance and not being able to smoke indoors. The only time I ever see him go three-quarters of an hour without a cigarette is when we watch football.

After the game the other Espanyol supporters clear out within ten minutes—Periquito isn't somewhere you hang out for the ambience, unless you're Ignacio—and once again we're outnumbered by the birds. Ignacio gets his cigarettes out and beckons me outside where he immediately lights up. All in all, I'm feeling pretty shite—I'd nursed one beer through the whole match, Ignacio is sulking, I'm still half-hungover and Beatriz hasn't responded to my text. It's not like I'm a teenager waiting on her, but if she is giving me the shoulder, it's going to make all the access code shite that much more difficult.

We sit down at a wonky plastic table and Ignacio takes a drag of his cigarette, leans back and unfurls like a flower catching the sun. Rosa, one of the bar staff, appears in her budgie t-shirt with a couple of beers. What the hell, as long as we avoid cocktails I'll be fine.

"I gotta talk to you, man," Ignacio says.

"You've had two hours."

He raises a calming hand. "We were watching the football."

"Yeah."

"I was asking some questions," he says. "The Russians."

I take a careful sip of my beer. "Why?"

"Last time, you know, I thought maybe you were involved with them."

"Not really. Not at all."

"Listen, these are bad people. I wouldn't have thought Hannah would touch them. If she's doing something for them, and you're helping her, you need to stop."

I reach for one of his cigarettes from the packet on the table.

"I thought you didn't," he says.

"Only on special occasions."

He flicks up his lighter and I take my own unsteady pull, feeling the rush flowing out from my chest.

"I would never have set you up with Hannah if I'd known," he says. "I thought it was just the kind of running around I did for her."

"You're scaring me, Ignacio." Also it's a flat-out lie. He'd known Hannah wanted someone with a specific background, so it's never been about parcel-drop offs and the like.

"These guys will fuck you up if you cross them, Tommy."

I take another drag. "Hannah said the same."

"If you can get out, my friend, get out. I heard the Russians had something big going down. You don't wanna be part of it."

I say nothing while I think. A fag is a great way of buying time. Ignacio is not a crook, exactly, but he knows some shady types. He's certainly better informed about the Russians than I am.

I put my glass down. "I've never met the Russians. I don't know the Russians. But I think they are Hannah's clients. And she's paid me. Quite a lot of money."

Ignacio narrows his eyes. "Give the money back. Walk away."

"Wouldn't that piss them off?"

He shrugs. "I don't know how deep you are with this. But if I was you, buddy, I'd give Hannah back the money, and I'd skip Barcelona for a few months. Maybe for good."

"This is my home."

"Nah. You might like it here, but it's a rich kid's game for you."

"Is that what you think?"

Ignacio stubs out his cigarette. "That you're a rich kid? Or you're playing?"

"If I was rich, why would I be working for Hannah? Or living in one room in Gràcia?"

"You're telling me you couldn't get on a plane tomorrow and go home?"

I stand up. "You've got the wrong idea about me, pal. I'm flat broke, I've got no publisher and no home in Scotland. It's here or nowhere. So if you're hanging out with me because you think I'm a trust fund brat, you've fucked yourself."

"Hey, I'm trying to help you, dude."

He slumps back in his seat and runs a hand through his hair.

"What are you not telling me?" I say as I stand over him.

He raises his hands defensively. "Don't put this on me."

"Fuck you, Ignacio. If you've got something to say, say it. Otherwise..."

He stands up clumsily, knocking his chair back. "No, fuck you, man. You just do your thing, see where it ends up. Seems like Carmen was right about you."

"Right about what?"

But I'm already talking to his back.

2

It's not that late when I get back to the flat—the metro was still open which saved me the hike back to Gràcia. I open the window and lean out over the street. What I said to Ignacio was true. There's nowhere else I can call home—certainly not Kilmarnock—and with its pulsing and sometimes anarchic energy, I love this city. Even this neighbourhood, far from affluent and well away from the city centre, has an ambience I've found nowhere else. I'm not going to let some hypothetical gangsters chase me back to Scotland.

I pour myself a glass of water and pad back to the window. Despite all that, I'm running out of rope here. The language classes are only part-time and I can't live off the money forever; I've burned through Kilpatrick & Robinson's advance. The only thing giving me a foothold here now is the money from Hannah—or more accurately, from the Russians.

I look down at my phone although I know there's nothing on it. No Beatriz means no progress on the job, but she hasn't responded. However much I enjoyed yesterday evening, she obviously didn't. Back to square one, if not further.

The clock on my phone flips over to midnight. Now it's

Thursday, and a banner comes up on the display: *Today's appointments: Social Club, 19-30, Broadway, c/de Montaner.* So much for not seeing Beatriz. I can picture the evening stretching ahead with excruciating embarrassment: fizzing silences, rancour, stilted small talk. Can I get away with not going? That's not going to wash with Hannah. If I want the money, I'm going to have to earn it. I'd always imagined a life of crime would be more glamorous than this

I eventually get to sleep about two a.m. and awake reasonably refreshed at nine. I busy myself in chores: some desultory cleaning, laundry and a trip to the supermarket. Coffee and the sports paper take up the rest of the morning—the correspondent had clearly watched a different Espanyol game to me—and then it's time for my afternoon class.

By the evening, I still haven't heard from Beatriz, but on the plus side Hannah is silent as well. I don't expect to hear from Ignacio, and he doesn't surprise me. Could he really have thought I was a wealthy expat? I'd given him credit for more discernment.

Seven p.m. comes around and I have to make a decision. I've seen t-shirts in the tat shops off the Ramblas with the slogan *Sorry I'm late, I didn't want to come.* If I had one, I'd have been tempted to wear it. Instead I opt for my second-best pair of jeans and a loose dark green shirt which had once lived in East Kilbride Marks and Spencer. We've both come a long way.

Under normal circumstances I'd be delighted to spend the evening at Broadway. It's altogether more upmarket than Periquito, and the mezzanine level even has a pool table where I can reliably hustle some money as long as I don't play Montse. I skip up the stairs with fake enthusiasm to find I'm the last to get there, and the others are all sprawled around a cluster of dark wooden tables pushed together.

"Tomàs!" calls Aleix. "We thought you weren't coming."

"Fashionably late," I say, with an attempt at nonchalance. The only free seat, inevitably, is next to Beatriz with Jaume on the other side. Tonight, this is the seating plan from hell.

Montse gets up to order some more drinks, and I consider stealing her seat on the end of one table next to Estel. This would to be hard to explain, and I know Montse harbours a particular dislike for Jaume—join the gang—so I sigh inwardly and sit down. Jaume gives me a brisk nod and Beatriz a perfunctory kiss on the cheek with sandpaper lips.

Luckily I don't have to say much. Estel is in a play at the Artesana premiering at the weekend and she has a torrent of observations on the theatre, her cast-mates and the lecherous director Alfonso. And she is undeniably funny, with an enjoyably malicious streak once she lets it off the leash.

I notice that Jaume engaging in some earnest flirtation with Salut on his other side, so at least he doesn't feel the need to bother waving his dick at me.

"How are you, Beatriz?" I say over the chatter of the bar, half-turned towards her.

She looks at me with melancholy brown eyes. "I am well, Tommy. And you?"

Shit, this is awful. And none of them except for Jaume call me anything but Tomàs anymore, a sign of acceptance in this Catalan group I only realise I miss now she's stopped doing it.

I pick up my beer glass before I realise it's empty and hold it halfway to my mouth while I work out what to do with it.

"I am well too," I say. "Really super super well."

Her lips quirk into an expression I can't read and she does

that pause I'd found so fascinating earlier in the week and now makes my guts roil.

"Good," she eventually says, and turns her attention back to Estel.

I notice her glass is empty too. "Do you want a drink?" I say in desperation. Because that went so well last time. She pauses, of course, as if it is a question of the utmost gravity. And in its way it is, I suppose.

She nods curtly. "*Gintonic.*"

After establishing that no-one else needs a refill, I slip away from the table with relief. Five minutes before I need to speak to her again. And perhaps I can commandeer the pool table after that.

As I stand at the bar, Estel eases up, hangs an arm around my shoulder. She looks at me with a thoughtful expression.

"I didn't think you wanted a drink," I say.

"I'm fine," she says, leaning towards me to be heard over the hubbub. She looks back across the room to where Beatriz is toying with the ice in her glass. "Beatriz is not herself tonight," she says.

This is undeniable. "She's certainly quiet," I say.

"I wonder why." Her eyes are fixed firmly on mine.

"I wouldn't know."

She puts a hand on mine. "I like you, Tomàs. I hope we are friends," she says. "And Beatriz is like my sister. Don't hurt her."

I tighten my lips. "I don't know what you mean."

She looks back at the tables to Jaume. "You do, Tomàs. And one dick in this group is enough."

With that she's gone. She was talking so much earlier that I'm amazed she's noticed anything else. One more thing to worry about. I've worked out enough about the dynamics of this group to realise that if Estel turns against me, I'm gone. Only the resolutely unsnubbable Jaume doesn't realise that.

Beatriz has thawed slightly by the time I bring the drinks over. "*Gràcies*," she says, smiling for the first time, although if I'm being critical it's not delivered with any conviction.

"*De res*. You're welcome. Have you seen Estel in a play before?" I say.

"Of course! She is much too good for the little theatre. All those years training and now she can't get any work. I hope someone will see her soon and she can give up the job in the office!"

"And would you like that too? To give up your job and make money from your art?"

She shrugs but at least she's looking at me. "I like my job," she says. "Although the pay is very bad. I don't have Estel's talent anyway."

"You know I like your work. Are you fishing for a compliment?"

She is almost smiling now. "I don't know what that means."

I can feel myself starting to relax. "It's like trying to catch fish. Except the fish are compliments."

"How would you do that? With a net? A rod?"

I grin. "The metaphor is not that exact. You have caught the compliment, anyway: I am sure lots of people would want to buy your work."

"If I can get my exhibition at the Petritxol, then people will buy it. But they still won't say yes."

Montse appears, to say goodnight. Her husband has flooded the flat and she needs to go home and fix the leak. I look at my watch and Beatriz glances at the display on her phone.

"It's late and I have to be at work early tomorrow," she says. "We have a rush job on."

"You didn't answer my text," I say before I can stop myself. Pause. More pause. She looks into my eyes with a depth I find terrifying.

At last she says: "I didn't know what to say."

"Anything would have done."

"I didn't know what you'd think of me. I'm not normally like that." She looks down into her glass.

"I thought you were someone who'd had one too many mojitos," I say. "And me as well. I hoped maybe there'd be a next time without mojitos at all."

She looks up. "*Ho sento.* I'm sorry. It's just—I'm confused. I don't know what I want."

"I know. You're repulsive. You told me."

Now she laughs. Next to me, Jaume stands up and jerks his head at Salut.

"Look," says Beatriz. "I promised I would give you the print, and I haven't. Come back with me and we'll get it now. I'm not drunk and I don't think you are either. It will be easier to talk away from here." Her gaze slides towards Jaume and Salut seemingly about to start an argument.

I can't see a downside to the suggestion.

"Come on," she says. "It's only a twenty-minute walk."

And as simply and unfathomably as that, she is Beatriz again.

3

EVERYONE STARTS TO DISPERSE, AND WE ALL MAKE OUR WAY ONTO THE pavements outside. The sun has gone and it's starting to get chilly.

Jaume has stalked off without further farewells, leaving Salut and Mèlia with their heads together in heated conversation. Montse is long gone to fix her plumbing.

"Let's go to Friends of Dorothy," says Aleix. "It's much too early to go home."

"Some of us have work tomorrow," says Beatriz.

"And if I'm not mistaken it's a gay bar," I say.

Aleix grins. "So? If you want to have a good time... you don't need to worry about your virtue if you're with me."

"Another night," I say.

Aleix turns to look at Estel, the only other person left.

"I love Friends of Dorothy," she says. "But I have a costume fitting before work tomorrow. We'll all go another time."

Aleix and Estel drift off towards the metro station.

"Are you coming?" says Estel. This early I normally wouldn't walk back to Gràcia. The metro is only a couple of euros.

"No, I'll walk. It's a nice night."

Estel shrugs. "Triz?"

"No, I'm walking too."

Estel silently eyes the pair of us. From Broadway, Beatriz lives south and I live north. Aleix watches the exchange and I see a light come on.

"Let's go, Estel," he says. "It's too cold to stand around here all night."

Estel nods and pulls her coat around her. "You're right. *Bona nit, Triz. Bona nit, Tomàs.*"

And with that the pair of them set off for the metro, leaving me alone with Beatriz on the pavement.

As we walk back to her flat, it's as if the previous awkwardness was a small hours anxiety dream. She is walking close, but not too close, and talking more than I have ever known her.

"Estel didn't seem delighted to see us going off together," I say as we arrive at her flat. Some North African kids are in the street playing hip-hop, and she gives them a quick smile and nod of recognition.

"She didn't actually see us go off," says Beatriz. "And anyway, she is very protective of me."

I laugh. "She doesn't need to protect you from me."

Pause. "Doesn't she?" Away from the streetlights her eyes are depthless pools. If there is emotion there I can't read it.

She manages the outer lock on the first attempt this time, and I follow her up the stairs. The door to her flat has an intricate and obviously expensive lock and I feel an unfathomable satisfaction that she is taking security seriously. Although a woman like that is unlikely to throw the Artesana access codes around like confetti.

I'm expecting her flat to be small and pinched like mine, because I can't imagine a graphic designer's salary stretches to much in the centre of Barcelona, even somewhere like the Raval. But of course it's nothing like mine.

For a start, it's properly lit, dimmable spotlights illuminating the pictures on walls—some of them clearly her own work—and creating inviting pools of shadow elsewhere. And although she has no less furniture than me, she's arranged it to convey an impression of light and airy spaciousness. It's almost minimalist but without the sterility.

"Sit down," she says, indicating a white leather sofa which proves more comfortable than its delicate frame suggests. "I'll make us some coffee."

She throws her leather jacket over the armchair, slips her shoes off and slides into the open plan kitchen. Given how nervy she's been so far, I'm expecting her to be even more wary now that we're alone together behind a locked door, but she's relaxed, keeping up a stream of chatter from the kitchen. This is home, and she feels safe here, even with me.

I look around as surreptitiously as I can to see if there might be a notepad where she's jotted down important details. She can't keep all those access codes in her head, surely—somewhere in the flat they must be written down. But if she has such a notebook, there's no sign of it in this clean and tidy space. And tonight, frankly, I can't be bothered with access codes.

She's out of milk and we drink our cheap coffee black. Now this, I think, truly is repulsive, and I take the smallest sips possible.

The sofa nominally seats two but it would be a tight squeeze. Instead she stays standing, leaning against the breakfast bar separating the kitchen from the living room.

"I'm sorry," she says, "that I didn't respond to your message."

"You said." I'm smiling. We're past that now.

She's come out of chatter mode. "I broke up with a guy. It

was horrible, I trusted someone I shouldn't have done and I got hurt."

Her expression turns inwards. For now, at least, I'm not there. She's forgotten that she'd mentioned this to me before.

"I'm sorry that happened to you," I say. "I know you didn't deserve it."

Her attention comes back. "The first time, you can't believe it, but it's not your fault. You know, you love someone and you think that's enough. And then you realise everything you thought about them was wrong."

I'm not sure I really want an unresolved break-up story, but if she wants to unload it, at least I can listen.

She divines what I'm thinking. She rubs her ear. "You don't want to hear about all that, and right now I don't want to talk about it. I just want you to understand why I don't find it easy to trust anyone. If it happens to me a second time, then it's my fault because I should know better. You seem like a good guy, Tomàs, a really good guy. But I am not going to rush into anything, no matter how much I like you."

I grimace at the bitterness of the coffee. I am so far away from being a good guy you couldn't measure the gulf. But here, with Beatriz, I wish I was.

She has retreated behind her eyes again. "Is that a problem for you? Because I don't know what you're thinking, but I'm not into casual."

I can't look at her. I'm supposed to get her to trust me, and perhaps I can, but afterwards... what is this going to do to her? It's all very well for me to say to Hannah that I didn't know any of these people, but I do now, and it's not so simple anymore. I can feel something juddering, and it's my conscience. I just can't do this. Tomorrow I'll text Hannah and give her back the money.

I get up and pour the remainder of my coffee down the sink.

"I'm not into casual either," I say. "And we have all the time we want."

A flush creeps into her cheeks.

"And next time I'm here..." I say.

She looks up.

"...I'm bringing some decent coffee."

She slips into what must be her bedroom and brings out the print and some tissue paper. I haven't seen it since the night of the exhibition, but I still love it. It's a high-res close-up of the iconic Fernando Botero bronze cat street sculpture, but she's only photographed half of its head, drawing in the rest with flowing black lines on a white background. The original sculpture is chubby and charming, but her drawing has given it a sinister and sensuous edge. I haven't described it very well, but if I could tell you about it in a sentence you wouldn't need to have made it. Anyway, I think it's completely beautiful, and that was before I thought the same about its creator.

I stand by the window and watch as she wraps and seals it in the tissue paper with astonishing speed and efficiency. Whatever she does, she does with complete absorption, whether it's wrapping a print or listening to what you have to say. Beatriz is not a multi-tasker.

She hands over the wrapped print. "For you," she says, kissing me on the cheek. She smells like summer. I badly want to kiss her back, and now I've binned off Hannah's scheme, why shouldn't I?

But she's just told me we're taking things slowly, and I can kiss her another day. She won't taste like an old ashtray.

"Thank you," I say. "It is a beautiful gift. Are you sure—"

"No, no. It's not for sale. I feel like I made it for you even though I didn't know you."

"I don't know what to say."

"Thank you was enough."

She's looking into my eyes and I'm going to ruin everything.

"I can't believe how quickly you wrapped that," I say to break the silence.

She laughs and throws herself down on the sofa.

"I spent a year in England on an exchange when I was at university. I worked in Tiffany's in London to help with the rent. You learned to wrap quickly there."

"You were in London?"

"Sure. 2005. Is it near Kil-mar-nock?"

I laugh. "No. In no sense is London anywhere near Kilmarnock. But strange to think we were in the same country for a year. Did you like it?"

She shrugged. "London was OK, although the weather was bad and everything was dirty. Tiffany's—foof!—all the other girls tried to steal your commission if you made a big sale. Every day was war."

My own experience of London, during my brief literary celebrity, had been fairly similar. "Better that we are here, now."

She just nods. Suddenly I'm feeling I ought to leave while I'm ahead. Once I can get clear of Hannah, this could be something wonderful.

"It's late," I say, and it is. Somehow we've been talking for two hours and I could never have told you any of it afterwards. "I should let you get some sleep."

She does the pause. I can't work out if she's relieved or disappointed. "I need to unlock the outside door for you."

I pick up the print and follow her down the stairs. She unlocks the door and we're out on the street. She's wrapped her arms around herself against the cold – after the warmth of the flat it's baltic out here.

"Don't wait out here," I say. "It's much too cold."

She retreats back inside the doorway.

I say, “Good n—”. She throws her arms around me and kisses me deeply. I was right: she doesn’t taste like an old ashtray. I kiss her back, but she skips back inside and shuts the grille behind her. She blows me a kiss and then she’s back up the stairs.

I hardly notice the walk back to Gràcia. I have a lot to think about. Once I get back to my flat I pull out my phone, which has been on silent, and plug it into the charger. There’s a text:

Bona nit, Tomàs. Bx

For some reason the words from the signs in the tat shops on the Ramblas come back to me. *You break it, you pay for it.*

PART FOUR
21 MARCH —17 MAY 2014

SWEET TIDES

I

I NO LONGER TEACH A CLASS ON FRIDAY; ATTENDANCE HAVING BECOME patchy. It hadn't occurred to the school that young adults might want to start their weekends early. I lounge in bed for a while, running over the previous evening with Beatriz. I have a free day, and one major errand to achieve. I text Hannah.

Need 2 meet urgently. Name time and place

Now it's just a question of waiting. I send Beatriz a text as well:

bon dia x

Today is the day I'm going to escape from all Hannah's shit. I won't have any money after this, but that's a different problem, and one I've managed to fudge so far. I've promised Polly an outline by the end of the month, and while I've as little desire to revisit Kilmarnock in fiction as I do in real life, I've been mulling over an idea for a fantasy novel instead. They don't strike me as particularly difficult to write, but I won't know until I try. There's always crime, of course, but that feels a bit close to home.

I brew some coffee on the stove, eat a croissant from yesterday and go for a long shower. I come back, towelling my hair, to three texts.

WTF is this, Chisholm? I set the meets.

We meet today or I'm out

This time Beatriz has responded too.

Bon dia. You want to go to the premiere of Estel's play tomorrow night? x

Of course. Txt me the details.

I'm glad not to be seeing her today. Put the rubbish out today, and by tomorrow I'm free and clear. No more lies, even ones of omission.

. . .

I don't recognise the third number.

We need to talk, Tomàs. You live in Gràcia, right? Meet me at the Greek theatre, Park Güell, 6 pm. Aleix.

I have no idea what Aleix wants to talk about, or indeed how he has my number. Park Güell, though, is only a quarter of an hour's walk from Baixada del Silur, plus another brief hike up through the woods. I look at my watch: plenty of time, although if Hannah wants to meet at the same time then Aleix is out of luck.

The phone pings. Hannah.

This had better be worth it.

U like the tourist spots. 6-30, Park Güell Greek Theatre

Her office is not that far away, and for once I have the upper hand. Let her come to me.

When I first moved to Barcelona, I visited Park Güell, a kind of Surrealist Disneyworld designed by Gaudí, all the time. If you're a local, it's free to get in, and since they started to limit visitor numbers, it's not too busy, even in the summer. Early evening in low season is even better—mainly couples crowding one side of the crazily tiled amphitheatre, looking out over the Gaudí cathedral and getting ready for the sun to set over the city. You get almost as good a view from the back, and there's no-one else there, so I perch on the wall to get my breath back after the steep climb and wait for Aleix. 17:56 – I've made good time.

As soon as I look up, I see Aleix springing down the stone steps towards me. He works out, jogs, and doesn't seem remotely out of breath. I've never known what his job is—he's been politely evasive whenever I've asked—and because he always dresses smartly I can't tell if he's come straight from the office or an afternoon doing whatever he does with his down-time. Today he's wearing a tailored jacket, skinny tie and pressed chinos with brogues. The bling he normally wears on a night out is carefully stowed away, but as ever, I feel under-dressed. He's brought two cardboard coffee cups with him. He hands one over and we shake hands.

We lean back against the buff stone wall and look out at the city set out below, the sea behind it and the light beginning to fade. Neither of us says anything for a few minutes as we sip our drinks.

"This is my favourite place in the city," he says eventually.

"A Gaudí fan?"

"Well, aren't we all? But I meant this spot, not the main park. The architecture palls after a while, you know? Seeing the city down there like that, though, puts everything in perspective. Not so big, not so important."

I've always loved this view as well, although I don't say so.

"Thanks for the coffee. It's good to meet up."

Aleix looks at me carefully. "You only saw me last night." He picks some lint from his sleeve.

"You don't always get to talk in the bar."

He turns away from the view and looks into the woods behind us.

"And there's something you want to talk about, Tomàs?"

"I don't pretend to know what this is about, and I'm very happy to meet, but I got the impression you wanted something. And as long as it's not money, I'll be delighted to oblige."

Aleix laughs and releases the crackling atmosphere. "How much do you know about Beatriz?"

The tension fizzes back into my shoulders.

"I don't know what you mean. Less than you, obviously."

"Last night, I got the impression..."

"What the fuck has this got to do with you, Aleix?"

He holds up a hand. "Steady, man. I don't mean you any harm here, OK. I'm just saying, it looked like you were going home with her last night."

I rip the cardboard sleeve off my coffee cup. "Like I said, Aleix. None of your fucking business."

Aleix sighs. "I'd like to think I'm friends with both of you. So maybe there are some things you should know."

"I don't know what you're trying to stir up here. She'd offered me one of her prints from the exhibition, and I went back with her to collect it. That's all, not that I have to explain anything to you."

"'Stir up'? For a straight guy, you seem pretty unprejudiced, but I don't appreciate you thinking all gay men do is make up bitchy gossip."

"You're the one who chose to interfere in my private life."

He pulls a packet of cigarettes out of his pocket. "Have you noticed how few guys there are in our little group?

"You, me, Jaume. Gonçal comes along sometimes."

He offers me a cigarette and lights one himself. "Jaume has run all the others off. He's not worried about me. You, I'm guessing he has a pretty major problem with."

"Can't say we talk much, right enough."

Aleix grins. "He wasn't always as bad as he seems now, or perhaps he was better at hiding it. He was always playing the sensitive guy, you know, good listener, eye contact, 'oh I feel your pain'."

"I know the type. 'Soft boi', we call them in Britain." It's not a million miles from what I'm doing myself.

"Obviously when he found himself in our little group he thought he'd gone to heaven. It wasn't long before he and Estel were an item."

This isn't where I'd imagined we were going. "Seriously? I'd have given her credit for more sense."

"It took us all a while to see through him. Estel didn't, but no-one else did either. They were together for nearly a year, and then she dumped him. There's a limit to how long you can keep your true self hidden."

He falls silent, perhaps reflecting on a similar event from his past.

"All that time," he continues, "Jaume liked everyone else's attention too. I gotta tell you, Beatriz had a bit of a thing for him."

This really is nothing to me, but a shiver runs down my spine. "So?"

"She and Estel are best friends, and Beatriz is the sweetest girl. So although that little shit flirted with her all the time he was with Estel, she didn't do anything about it, except maybe mope a bit."

"You got a cigarette?"

He passes one over and lights it.

"And then, of course, Estel and Jaume broke up. And Beatriz, she was so into him that within a couple of weeks they'd got together instead."

I concentrate my attention on the cigarette's glowing end. It feels wrong to be having a conversation like this in such glorious surroundings.

"Sorry if this is painful," he says.

"It's not. Carry on."

"In her heart she knew what he was like, but she couldn't do anything about it. We've all had crushes like that, right?"

"Speak for yourself."

"Whatever, man. Anyway, Beatriz had waited a year to be with Jaume, and within six weeks it was over. He cheated on her, tried to make out she'd driven him to it."

"Shit. Poor Beatriz."

"Yeah. Not pretty at all."

I say nothing.

"There's two things you need to understand," he continues. "First, she's not really over it. This was only last autumn. Second, she's not ready to trust someone else. I don't think she will for a long time."

"Thanks for telling me. I don't know why it affects me."

Aleix is the most smooth and urbane of men. But he leans in closer to me and his eyes are alight.

"Don't fuck with her, Tomàs. She doesn't deserve it."

"Don't fuck with, or don't fuck?" I'm losing patience with this sanctimonious bullshit.

Aleix draws back. "I hope I wasn't wrong about you. Beatriz is a good friend, and I don't want to see her hurt. I'm asking you not to do it."

There's something about Beatriz which attracts this protective loyalty: Xabi in El Gat, Estel, Aleix now. And yet I think there's an underlying toughness in her which doesn't need it. Or maybe I'm kidding myself.

"Nothing's happened between us, Aleix. I appreciate the

appeal to my better nature, but she's a grown woman and she can make her own decisions."

Aleix runs a hand through his gelled hair. "This—advice, if you want to call it that, —is for your good too. There's no possible happy ending here."

"There's not even been a beginning, pal, so there can hardly be an ending."

He nods and throws his empty cup in the waste bin. "I've said what I came to say, Tomàs. The rest is up to you."

He turns and sets off down the hill.

I don't know how long I brood into the view of the city set out below. I can just about make out Baixada del Silur; Carrer del Tigre is too far off to pick out.

I hear footsteps on the ground behind me.

"Who was that?"

I turn to see Hannah.

"No-one you'd know. Not everything in my life is your schemes."

Hannah, in a work suit today, shrugs. "He didn't look very happy. It's almost as if you have a talent for pissing people off, Chisholm. Maybe it's the Scottish cantankerousness."

"Thanks for coming, anyway," I say. "There, I can be nice."

"You didn't give me much choice." She indicates her suit. "I don't appreciate being dragged out of the office early or having to walk up this fucking hill."

"You should maybe cut down on the fags."

"For someone who wants a favour, you have an odd way of going about it."

"I'm not asking you. I'm telling you." I reach into my jacket pocket and pull out the envelope. "There's your ten grand. I'm out."

She smiles and shakes her head, leaning on the wall as Aleix had done.

"Out?"

"Just take the fucking money. This is finished. Find someone else to do your dirty work."

She turns her head to look at me as I lean next to her. "You can't imagine it's that simple."

"You paid me to do a job. I can't do it and I won't do it. Here's your money, except for the thousand euros I paid the rent with, and I figure I've earned that."

"You are like a fucking teenager. You've fallen in love with one of those Spanish sluts, haven't you?"

"No."

"I've heard more convincing denials. For Christ's sake, Chisholm! You can't trust a man to do anything without fucking it up."

"Look, I've come to like them—all of them. I won't exploit them for some Russian fucking gangsters."

She gives a bleak smile. "It's the gangsters who are the problem," she says more softly than I'd expected. "I don't care who you're sleeping with or what you feel about them. But the Russians want those paintings. They are not patient and they are not reasonable. If this doesn't happen, they will hurt you. I'm not too bothered about that either, but when they come after me, that's when I get—agitated."

"Look, Hannah, just find another way. You'd have done something else if Ignacio hadn't introduced us."

Her blue eyes are steady as she looks into mine. "Tommy, this is big league now. I'm sorry I didn't tell you that to begin with, but there we are. You can't back out now. Just do the job, collect the money, and you'll have a plot for your next novel."

"You think I'd write about this? You're mad. I just want to pretend it never happened."

Her laugh has a bitterness not previously apparent. "We all

get there eventually. You push through it, and on the other side you see it's no big deal."

"I'm not sure I want to be the kind of person who sees seducing and abandoning a woman for profit as 'no big deal'."

She pats my chest where I'd tucked the envelope back into my breast pocket. "Too late. Welcome to the dark side. Now do your fucking job."

2

Back in my flat, I make a dismal meal and reflect on the complete failure of my plan. The chance to let a normal relationship with Beatriz develop is gone. Already I'm in too deep to confess to her, even without her now understandable trust issues.

I wonder about the Russians. I don't mix in the underworld and I've never heard of them. They can't be international super-criminals with a reach across the whole of Europe, surely? They're obviously big players in Barcelona—Ignacio knows of them and they scare him. Their tentacles can't possibly stretch to Kilmarnock if I want to run that far, though. I heard enough when I lived there about various local hard-men and their connections to think there wouldn't be room for southern European gangsters who could have no conceivable interest in the town.

But the last thing I want to do is run to Kilmarnock. The whole reason I'm here is to escape it, and I'm doing pretty well at it, if you ignore the lack of cash and precarious job.

I spent a month the first summer I was here in a tiny village high in the Alpujarra mountains, fleeing the August heat in the city. It's almost completely off the grid, and the chances of the Russians tracking me there, even if they can be bothered, are remote. I can't stay there forever, though, and I certainly can't ask a city girl like Beatriz to come with me. And already that matters. The solitude of the mountains was invigorating for a month, but I can't imagine it for much longer.

I can stay in Barcelona and call their bluff, of course. Hannah is their mouthpiece and they might well vent their displeasure on her, but surely I'm too small a fish to be worth bothering with. If they want the paintings that badly, they'll come up with another way, or lean on Hannah to.

I brew myself a pot of decent coffee and drink it from a cracked Espanyol mug, looking out of the window onto the lively street below. The more I think about it, the more I know it won't work. For whatever reason, the Russians want the paintings. They won't give up, and I know about the plan. Once I'm outside of it, I become a dangerous loose end, able to report them to the police beforehand, or lead them to Hannah afterwards. They can't afford to leave me running around Barcelona knowing as much as I do.

If I'm not prepared to run—and I'm not ready to yet—then the only remaining option, the ugly option, is to continue with the plan. Do whatever I need to do to get Beatriz to give me the tools to unlock the Artesana. If nothing else, it buys me time. I haven't actually done anything that bad until I hand the access codes over to Hannah. Until that point, nothing has crystallised. It's still an imaginary crime. Do I really believe that? It almost doesn't matter. It's enough to keep me spending time with Beatriz, winning her confidence and enjoying her company.

There's nothing I'm doing with her just now—drinks, coffee at her flat, a visit to the theatre—that I wouldn't have done anyway given a free choice. I like her a lot more than I ever did

Carmen, and no-one had to pay me to sleep with her. Beatriz and I might become more intimate, but that too is hardly something I need coercion to pursue. She's worried that I'll lie about my feelings and break her heart at the end of it; so if I'm not lying about my feelings, it's not really a breach of trust. OK, it's not an argument that could stand up to the closest scrutiny, but it's not complete bollocks either. And who knows, it gives me time to come up with a solution which gets us both out free and clear.

I finish my coffee. I ache with wanting to see her. Aleix playing the big brother and Hannah the big bad bitch doesn't change that. But I'll see her tomorrow and it's worth showing some restraint now. It would be ironic if she becomes so wearied of me that she starts keeping her distance. I settle for sending a text saying I miss her and am looking forward to the play. I also send her a photograph of the print in its new home, although it's far too grand for the seedy bachelor flat.

I'm at a loose end for the rest of the evening, so I decide it might be time to make up with Ignacio, if only to see if I can learn more about the Russians. I text him to apologise for the row, although the fault is entirely his. Perhaps I'm getting the hang of the manipulation game. But he doesn't respond and I spend the evening in the flat.

3

MUCH AS I LOVE BARCELONA, THE QUIRKY VIBRANCY, THE extraordinary architecture, the climate, the bustle, it's a while since I've had a Saturday night out here with a pretty girl. Carmen, probably, but let's not go there. Ideally I might not have chosen Catalan regional theatre as the vehicle, but it's the company that's important, and I can't imagine anyone I'd rather be with than Beatriz.

Tonight she is wearing a sleeveless burgundy blouse, a suede miniskirt and heels that make her taller than me, even though I'm five-ten. Bangles clatter on her wrists and pendant dolphin earrings hang level with her jaw. Her red hair is polished to an industrial sheen, and even in the dusk her eyes sparkle with liquid brilliance.

"How much of this am I going to understand?" I say as we wait in the queue. The Artesana foyer doors are already open so I'm not going to learn anything about their access codes today. "You know my Catalan is unimpressive."

"You'll be fine," she says. "The story is not complicated. Besides, we are here to support Estel."

"I know, but I don't want to say anything wrong to her afterwards because I couldn't follow what was going on."

She kisses me on the cheek. "You are very tactful, Tomàs."

"It's more that I fear her wrath if she thinks I wasn't paying attention."

She laughs. "You would not want to face her wrath! She is a demon. I will explain the plot before we go backstage if you missed anything."

We collect our tickets. I notice that the main gallery is locked and I see, for the first time, a couple of discreet CCTV cameras. I wonder if Beatriz would know how to turn those off even if she were minded to tell me.

The play proves to be a pile of old shite, right enough. The plot seems to consist of a series of increasingly strident quarrels arising from no basis I can understand. The quality of the acting is also indifferent—the required histrionics seeming to magnify most of the actors' tendency to overact. The one exception is Estel, who amidst the chaos of indolent direction, forgotten lines and missed cues, shows a talent far in excess of everything else on display. The subtle restraint of her own performance is enhanced by the ranting all around her. I imagine that in a fully professional production surrounded by competent actors, she'd be extraordinary. I take a curious and unwarranted pride in her achievement. Beatriz, who has held my hand throughout the play, is beside herself with excitement.

The players appear for their curtain call and an ovation which far exceeds their merits. The director appears for his own bow: neither the cast nor the audience has anything to thank him for, but he feasts on their acclaim. In his preening acceptance of his due I see a man steeped in self-regard, and as he rests his hand on Estel's buttocks, a displeasing lechery. If Beatriz has noticed she says nothing.

The audience files out in respectful silence, but we have arranged to meet Estel backstage. She and Beatriz shriek and embrace. I kiss her on both cheeks in more restrained fashion.

"Congratulations," I say. "You were astonishing, really!"

She takes both my hands. "*Gràcies*, Tomàs! And did you like the play?"

"Ah, of course! It was..." My ingenuity fails me, and anyway, if I overpraise it, I devalue the genuine appreciation I expressed for her performance.

Beatriz rescues me. "It was in Catalan, and it may have been a struggle for poor Tomàs."

She hugs both of us and looks round furtively. The director, Alfonso, is nowhere in sight and she whispers: "You don't have to flatter us. It was terrible. I am only hoping that some of the critics notice I was not quite so bad as the rest."

"Honestly, Estel, you were the only one who looked like a real actor," I say.

This seems to delight both her and Beatriz, although the remark was surely self-evident. Estel has outlined the flaws of her cast-mates on several previous occasions.

She leads us both into the cubby which is her own changing area, and she starts to swab off her make-up. She beckons us to sit down on the narrow bench next to her seat. Looking at us out of the mirror, she says:

"So, you two..."

This could be an awkward conversation. Estel has been clear, with me at least, in her opposition. And that's before we get on to Jaume, about whom I'm not supposed to know.

Beatriz squeezes my hand. "Yes, us two."

Estel's eye flicks towards me in the mirror. I'm sure we're both thinking about the conversation in Broadway.

"Tomàs, I hope you know how lucky you are," she says with a lightness that doesn't reach her eyes.

"Well, I would never have got to see a masterpiece of contemporary Catalan theatre otherwise."

Beatriz laughs and leans against me. Estel seems less enraptured.

"It's no big deal," I say. "We're just spending some time together."

I don't know how that will go down with Beatriz, because I still have only the haziest impression about her feelings. Her hand twitches on mine.

At this moment, Alfonso puts his head around the door, flushed with his triumph. He has the kind of stringy good looks and bumptiousness that I imagine Jaume might grow into in twenty years.

"Don't forget we are going out to celebrate, Estel!" he beams. "You were magnificent."

He approaches as if to embrace her. "Ten minutes, Alfonso. I'm talking to my friends."

Alfonso doesn't look to be interested in Estel's friends, for which I'm grateful. Beatriz gives him a look of unconcealed loathing. He oozes back out of the dressing area.

"Sorry about that," Estel says. "The cast is going out for dinner. I'd invite you but I don't think you'd enjoy it. I'm sure you can find better ways to amuse yourselves."

Before I can respond to that, Beatriz says: "Alfonso! Foof! Is he still...?"

Estel makes an expression suggesting she has a bad taste in her mouth. "Of course."

"He is old enough to be your father! I don't know how to describe him—he is..." says Beatriz.

"Repulsive," I say with a smile. Beatriz gives me a wondering expression.

"I can take care of myself," says Estel. "He thinks being a director means he can fondle the actresses."

"Repulsive," repeats Beatriz.

Estel sighs. "It's the price you pay. If I'd slapped him the first time, he'd have stopped but I wouldn't have got the part."

I am genuinely outraged at this behaviour. I'd always imagined tales of the casting couch to be exaggerated. Something of this comes through in my tone as I say: "See that guy, someone should give him a smack."

Estel's lips curl into a smile. "Are you volunteering?"

"Do you want me to? I know a couple of people who might oblige." This isn't strictly true, but I imagine Ignacio does, if we make up from our quarrel. Maybe Hannah could even lay on some Russians.

"Tomàs, you are the most unlikely feminist!" trills Estel.

Beatriz is quietly eyeing the exchange. "I don't think Tomàs would hit somebody," she says. She's formed an impression of my character based on limited information, but as so often she's right. In Kilmarnock sometimes you had to square up to the local neds, but out here it's easier just to go with the flow.

"If I can't handle Alfonso myself," Estel says, "I'm in the wrong job."

Alfonso soon reappears to chivvy Estel along. He still hasn't acknowledged Beatriz or me, which is fine with both of us. Estel gathers up her kit and says her farewells to us. As she kisses me on the cheek, she whispers into my ear: "Now you are the great feminist, Tomàs, make sure you respect Beatriz."

I don't have time to respond before she's gone. I'm starting to get annoyed with all her friends warning me to behave properly, as if I'm some unprincipled seducer. They're right, of course, but that's not the point: they're acting like I'm that wee shite Jaume when I've given them no reason to think so.

"What did Estel say to you?" asks Beatriz.

"Nothing. Just 'have a nice evening'."

We stroll out of the theatre. Inwardly I'm noting the position of a couple of CCTV cameras I missed on the way in. "Have you been in the gallery?" I say. "Apparently there's an exhibition of Llorenç Llussàs in the summer."

"There's not normally much to see," she says. "The Llussà exhibition is out of the ordinary for us. He's not an artist people pay attention to these days, but he was influential in the Franco times."

"You're an expert?"

"Professional interest," she says. "He's not one of my influences but I like to be aware of what the Catalan artists have done."

"We should go and see them in the MACBA one day," I say. I'd like to have a sense of what all the fuss is about.

She beams. "I didn't think you were interested in art," she says. "You're only saying it to impress me."

"If you'd like to go, so would I. I'm sure I'll learn something."

We step outside into the night air. It's distinctly chilly now and Beatriz slips on her leather jacket. I look at my watch and see it's not that late: the play had felt far longer than its hour and a half run-time. I ask her if she wants to go for a drink.

"Do you mind? I'm really tired," she says.

So that's how it's going. "OK. If you want to call it a night, that's fine." How polished my manners are.

"I'm not that tired," she smiles. "Where do you live?"

"Gràcia. Baixada del Silur – just south of Park Güell."

"Catfish Alley!" she exclaims delightedly.

"Uh?" I'm known for my sparkling repartee.

"That's what Baixada del Silur means in English. Catfish Alley. Didn't you know?"

"You've heard my Catalan. If I can tell a *gat* from a *gos* I'm doing well." This is a—slight—exaggeration. I can just about remember the words for cat and dog, particularly as El Gat Blau is her favourite bar.

"I like the sound of Catfish Alley," she says. "But Gràcia is miles away. Why don't we go back to Carrer del Tigre, have a coffee and listen to some music."

"Tiger Street?" I smile, even my Catalan being up to this translation.

She slips an arm through mine. "Come on. I'm freezing!"

Idly I wonder how a girl who thinks a fourteen-degree evening is cold would ever have fared in Kilmarnock.

4

It's only the second time I've been inside Beatriz's flat but already I feel worryingly at home. Mentally I decide to park access codes for the rest of the evening. In keeping with my new rule, this is how I would have chosen to spend the night anyway so I needn't feel guilty. So I don't, much.

She reappears from the concealed corner of the kitchen, holding a bottle of red wine and two glasses. "I have this if you'd prefer. You didn't like the coffee last time."

"Eroski is the worst coffee on the planet," I say, although as someone who grew up with Mellow Birds I know this isn't true. "I'd have brought some Bonka if I'd known we were coming here."

It's perhaps for the best that the bilingual pun escapes her. It's hardly shown my wit at its most scintillating. And I prefer Café Bustelo anyway.

"I buy better wine than coffee," she says with a half-smile. "You want to try it?"

"I should test if that's true."

She sets the bottle and glasses down on the breakfast bar.

She fills both and hands one to me. Her fingers brush mine and she tucks her hair behind her ear.

She doesn't say anything. I walk over to the balcony, open the door and step out. There's room, just, for both of us and we stand looking at the knots of people passing in the street, only a few feet below us. The streetlights bring out the copper in her hair and cast her eyes in pools of shadow. It's Saturday night in one of the world's most vibrant cities, and we could be the only people in the world.

If she knew how I'd come to be here... I push the thought away. The time for that is gone.

She transfers her glass to her left hand, and rests her right on top of mine on the railing. In the chill evening air, her skin is impossibly warm. I can feel the heat radiating from her. I have one last chance to do the right thing, to walk away and never look back. But I can't; I've already let her get too close; I'm caught in her gravity. Her lips are slightly parted. She says "Tomàs, let's go back inside. It's cold out here," and she takes my hand.

I set my glass down and gently touch her cheek. The time for words is past.

I wake the next morning to find the sun leaking past the shutter. Beatriz is still asleep next to me, lying on her front with her tattooed arm sprawled across me. I slide out, pull my shirt on, go to the bathroom and then put the kettle on.

I peer through the kitchen blinds while I wait for the coffee to brew. Last night has shaken so much loose in my mind. I know now, if I hadn't already, that being with Beatriz is the most important thing in my life. And even better, if that's possible, I've realised something about the Russians: no-one, other than Hannah and Ignacio, has ever heard of them. These shadowy underworld figures, who presumably spend their days organising prostitution and people-smuggling, have now moved into art theft? Where's the mileage for them in that? They'll never be able to sell them on.

The truth, now I've realised it, is almost too obvious. There are no Russians. There never were. Only Hannah and Ignacio, looking for someone to get them into the Artesana. Grubby eastern European crooks might not be able to shift the Llussàs, but I'll bet shady Hannah, bent international lawyer to the rich and unscrupulous, with her villa in Sant Cugat—she can fence them on, right enough.

I'm free and clear. I just have to tell her to fuck off, and with no Russians on the scene, she's got no leverage at all. If I'm wrong, no doubt the Russians will make themselves known. But I'm not wrong.

"Tomàs!" she calls out from the bedroom. "Are you there?"

"Sorry if I woke you. I'm making coffee."

I bring the drinks through and get back into bed.

"I thought for a moment you'd gone," she says, a hand on my thigh.

"After last night?" I laugh. "You'll need a bulldozer to get rid of me." Especially now I've worked out how to deal with Hannah.

She leans her head against me. "I didn't know if you would still feel the same way today. Men are not always..."

I'd managed not to think about men's characters, specifically my own, for twelve hours. But all the old problems are still here.

"What is it?" she asks.

I shake my head. "It's nothing. Last night was wonderful, you are wonderful. I'd like it if we could..."

She raises her eyebrows. "Now?"

"That wasn't exactly what I meant, but if you insist..."

Later, she slips on my shirt and pads across to the window to adjust the shutter. Soft light leaks in through the thin voile curtain.

"I'm hungry," she says. "Let's go and have lunch."

I've no idea what time it is—it could as easily be breakfast time—but we've had nothing to eat since before the theatre last night.

"Sure," I say. "Although you're wearing my only shirt."

She laughs and flicks it off over her head in a single graceful movement. Lunch has immediately become less interesting.

She comes and sits next to me on the bed, her shoulder against my chest. "I don't know anything about you, Tomàs."

My smile feels more like a grimace. "Of course you do. What more do you need to know? I'm a writer, I'm from Scotland, and I prefer it here in Barcelona. For lots of reasons. There's nothing else interesting to say."

She rolls away so that she can inspect me from a distance. Her eyes are large with a melancholy expression. "Last night, it meant something, yes?"

"You know it did."

"Then I want to know about you. All about you. Don't you want to know about me?"

I laugh uneasily. "Of course I do, Beatriz." I try for a lightness of tone I don't feel. "But you've already told me everything."

She frowns. "You think I talk too much?"

I run a hand through my hair and squirm under the sheets. "I didn't mean that. But I'd rather listen than talk. All writers are like that."

"So you're going to put me in a book?"

This time my laugh is genuine. "No way. This is just for us."

She takes my hand. "Why do you hate Scotland so much?"

Her legs are crossed in front of me, and I trace with my finger the outline of an Espanyol tattoo on her ankle.

"I can tell you've never been there," I say easily. "Nine months of rain a year, half an hour a day of sunshine if you're lucky. And no Beatriz."

Her eyes are sad. "Don't do that."

"Do what?"

"Make a joke of it. I'm being serious. Don't you trust me enough to tell me anything important?"

I sigh and lean back against the pillow. "It's no secret. It's just not very interesting, and it's not a feel-good story."

She runs a finger along my jaw. "You can still tell me. But you don't have to if it upsets you."

See, the less I have to think about Kilmarnock, the better. I've never spoken to anyone here about it, and I can still slide out of it now. But it's been my job since February to build an intimacy with Beatriz, and this will help. It's not my job anymore, it's real life, but for reasons I don't really understand, I do want to tell her about it.

"You need to understand," I say. "Kilmarnock really is a shithole. Endless bleak, depressing poverty, no ambition, just one fucking day after another all the same, all just waiting for something to happen. And when it does, it's usually bad."

Her attention is rapt on my face. A smudge of mascara from yesterday is clumped in one corner of her eye.

"And I could have dealt with that, growing up in it and not

knowing anything better. My dad worked in the carpet factory until he got laid off. He could never get another job, it was all call centres and IT. He didn't understand any of that stuff and he didn't want to know."

Beatriz squeezes my hand.

"There were hundreds, even thousands, of families in Kilmarnock like us. We weren't unusual. Where we were different was that my mum was a teacher. A grim school, the one that I went to, Arthur Bain Academy. The other kids hated me because I was a teacher's son, but my mum was the head of the English department. So I discovered books, reading my way into other worlds that weren't Kilmarnock. And then I found out that I could write as well, and I realised how I could get out of Kilmarnock for real, not just in my head. From that moment, I was always going to be a writer."

Beatriz catches her lower lip with her teeth. "So maybe it wasn't so bad."

I shake my head. I don't want to go here, and I've hardly thought about it for fifteen years. Maybe I've just been waiting for the right person to tell.

"When I was fourteen, my mum was diagnosed with lung cancer. She was only forty-three, but she was a heavy smoker, both my parents were. It was an aggressive form, and she'd put off going to the doctors for so long that by the time they found it, they couldn't do anything." I swallowed. "She was dead inside a year."

Beatriz's mouth drops open in soft horror. She cradles my head in her arms. "I'm so sorry," she whispers. "I didn't mean to bring all this up."

"It's OK," I whisper. "I'm glad I've told someone, and I'm glad it was you."

She's crying now. I'm not. Any emotion I had about it is long since scorched out.

"My dad started drinking—even more, I mean. My sister was eighteen, and got married and divorced within two years. My dad insisted I left school at sixteen so that I could get a job at the Vodafone call centre, the height of his ambition for me. I refused and slept on a friend's sofa for two years while I did my Highers. My grades were good enough for university, and that was Kilmarnock and me finished forever. And the only time I ever revisited it was in my head, when I wrote *Fear and Loathing in Kilmarnock*."

"Oh, Tomàs..."

"Sorry," I say with a bright smile. "You did ask."

She puts her arms around me and we sit in silence on the bed. Her warmth and soft scent give me a peace that I hadn't realised I was missing.

Refreshed after taking a shower together, we go out for lunch. Now that we've established that last night wasn't a transient impulse, we're both more relaxed. And if she'd had any doubts, me telling her about Kilmarnock had settled them. We'd never have to refer to it again, but it had crossed a bridge for both of us. I'd kind of hoped that sleeping with Beatriz would have got her out of my system, which would hurt both of us less in the long run. But it hasn't been like that at all. It's brought us closer together, and now I can see the way out, I'm briefly tempted to be honest about the whole thing. I don't need to worry about access codes anymore. But she'll never trust me again. All the time there's a chance of my getting out from this without her knowing, I have to keep my own counsel.

"Tomàs?" She rests a hand on mine. "Are you listening to me?"

"Sorry." I grin. "I was just thinking about last night." Which is not untrue.

She playfully bats my hand. “I can’t take you out at all!”

I push my thoughts aside as she continues to tell me about her forthcoming meeting with the curator of Galeria Petritxol, where she is still hoping to have an exhibition, and I listen with an interest which is no longer feigned.

5

I'VE NEVER BEEN TO THE OLD ROMAN CITY OF TARRAGONA BEFORE, although it's less than an hour from Barcelona, but this weekend Beatriz and I have driven up. We've been a couple for maybe six weeks. Two of her friends from university, Vicenç and Júlia, are getting married. At least one of their families has money, because they've hired the twelfth-century Castell de Claramunt, a few kilometres outside the town and overlooking the sea.

"Are you sure you want to take me?" I'd said the first time she mentioned it. "We haven't been together very long."

The supermarket is maybe not the place to have this conversation, but you play the ball where it lies.

Beatriz is scrutinising the vegetables with more care than they deserve. "Of course. Why wouldn't I? Unless you—"

This is no time to have an attack of guilt. And I've got nothing to feel guilty about anyway. I haven't heard anything from Hannah since I'd sent her a note weeks ago telling her I was out, so as far as I'm concerned, the heist is off. Beatriz and I are just girlfriend and boyfriend. And if she wants to show me off to all her old friends, that's fine with me.

I take out two of the three packs of tomatoes she has absent-mindedly put in the trolley. "I'd love to go," I say. If nothing else, this will be different to a Scottish wedding, and in fact the first time I've been to one without having to wear a kilt.

Castell de Claramunt is undeniably a fairytale castle, and Beatriz is simmering with excitement as we walk up the grand outdoor staircase. She's taking the event very seriously; only with difficulty have I talked her out of wearing a hat, and she's insisted I wear a tie for the first time since school. I ought to be irritated, or at least superior, but I'm not. There's something about her simple unfeigned delight that disarms anything else I might be feeling. She's wearing a knee-length burgundy dress with a single shoulder strap that exposes most of her back. I'd bought her a Paloma Picasso olive-leaf gold pendant from Tiffany on Passeig de Gràcia, in tribute to her year working in the London store. She's thrilled with it. If I think about it too hard, I can't escape the fact that it was bought with Hannah's money, so I choose not to think at all. I just admire it in its perfect setting.

"Oh!" she breathes as we reach the top of the steps, to reveal a panoramic view out over the sea and the village below. Tarragona itself nestles away in the distance. She whips out her camera and takes a series of shots. "I am going to make a collage from this when we get home."

"Always the artist," I smile.

"Doesn't this inspire you to write something?"

"I never write about nice things." The fantasy novel I

outlined and sent to Polly needs a castle, and this will do very well as a model, but since that ends up destroyed with its inhabitants slaughtered, I keep my thoughts to myself.

A cry comes out of the walled garden. “Beatriz!”

She turns and shrieks in return. “Mar!”

She runs over to embrace her friend, a short black-haired woman her own age with a toddler at the end of each arm. Next to her stands a tall man in fashionable glasses. He’s introduced as Artur, the infants as Felip and Iris.

Mar pushes her sunglasses up to inspect me. “So this is the famous Tomàs!” She kisses me on both cheeks. “We’ve heard so much about you.”

I give Beatriz a side-glance. “Is that so?”

She gives an apologetic smile. “I might have mentioned you in emails a couple of times.”

“Tsss!” says Mar. “She talks about nothing else, except for her pictures!”

I find this, too, less annoying than I might have done.

Mar and Beatriz had been great friends at university, and accordingly we have all been seated at the same table, under the dappled shade of a lemon tree. I generally dislike children, and I have no idea how old these two are, although they’re clearly twins. Two? Three? So far, at least, they seem relatively docile, but sugar will be coming later and I doubt they will add to the day’s enjoyment once they become over-stimulated. This is my one decent suit, so I hope they don’t puke on it. Beatriz seems to have no similar concerns about her designer dress.

For now, though, sipping cava and watching Beatriz and Mar catch up on gossip, I’m feeling pretty mellow. Artur is pleasantly taciturn; he has some mind-numbing finance job with the Spanish government in Madrid, which mercifully he is disinclined to discuss. The breeze takes the edge off the heat and I'd be quite happy to sit here all day, but at some stage there's going to be a wedding.

As if on cue, we are gently rounded up and herded towards rows of seats by someone Beatriz tells me is the bride's brother. Because our party has young children we get to sit at the back, presumably in case screaming or tantrums require their exfiltration at short notice.

The groom, Vicenç, is sitting in the front row and even from this distance I can see his legs jumping with nerves. Why would anyone put themselves through this? Fortunately he does not have long to wait, for within a couple of minutes the bride, Júlia, appears, clutching her father's arm. Beatriz and Mar both make an identical gasp at the sight of Júlia's dress, which to me looks like a pretty standard wedding gown—although apparently she has designed it herself. Beatriz bursts into tears and clutches my hand, and I pass over my packet of tissues.

It's certainly an attractive scene, the couple standing before a floral arch with the sea behind them. I don't know how much of it Beatriz or Mar take in, since they both sob their way through the ceremony. Iris and Felip, at least, don't upset the script.

"Wasn't that beautiful?" says Mar as we file our way back to our table afterwards. "Beatriz, you remember our wedding, that ratty little *Registro Civil* opposite the supermarket."

Artur shifts Iris in his arms and raises an eyebrow. "You were the one who insisted on a quick wedding! And we could never have afforded somewhere like this!"

This has the feel of a long-rehearsed argument.

Mar puts Felip down. "Anyway, this must have given you some ideas, Beatriz?"

Beatriz gulps. "Well, I hadn't really—"

Mar punches her arm. "You can't tell me that you come to

one of your oldest friends' wedding in a place like this and you don't think about your own!"

"Mar!" Beatriz gives her a pleading look, failing to conceal either the blush or involuntary side-glance at me. "Now isn't the time—"

"Oh, look!" cries Mar. "Now you have upset poor Tomàs."

"Really," I say. "There's no—"

"Do you have to, Mar?" says Artur with a weary expression. "You hardly know Tomàs and you are embarrassing them both."

We reach our table and I instinctively hold out Beatriz's chair for her to sit down.

"I'm only playing!" laughs Mar. "I'm sure Beatriz is able to make her own plans without me."

Artur gloomily subsides into his own seat.

"Although," continues Mar, "Tomàs is *very* handsome and obviously a gentleman!"

"Mar!" shout Artur and Beatriz in unison.

She holds up her hands. "All right, all right! I can tell no-one is in the mood for love today, which is a shame at a wedding."

She leans forward to me and says in a stage whisper "Although Tomàs, I will just observe that no woman, ever, would say no to being married in a castle. Just in case that information comes in useful one day."

Beatriz is laughing now. "Mar, you are impossible!"

The arrival of a uniformed waiter with cava, who makes a play of offering a drink to the two children, is undeniably well timed.

I've always noticed at upmarket venues like this, that the posher and more elaborate the presentation of the food, the less of it there is. Here there are all kinds of seafood served on what appear to be roof slates, and none of it touches the sides. I find myself envying the plainer fare presented to Iris and Felip, which at least seems to match their appetite. Despite the shortage of food, the time skips past and, as evening begins to fall, I realise I'm enjoying myself. Mar has reined in her comments about weddings and is both kind and amusing. Artur bears her flights of fancy with the ease of long practice, and when the children start to get restless, it is Beatriz who kicks off her high heels and kneels on the grass to play with them, entertaining them with ludicrous noises and gestures, tossing them up into the air and catching them.

An area has been cleared on the grass for an informal dance-floor, and as the sun begins to set a DJ appears to begin his set. Vicenç and Júlia have their first outing as a married couple, Beatriz holding up a fascinated Iris for a better view.

Mar takes my hand. "While your girlfriend is looking after my children," she says, "you can show me how well you dance."

"Not very, and surely Artur would—"

Artur airily waves his cigarette at me. "Please, Tomàs, do as she says, or I will get no peace!"

I catch Beatriz's eye and she grins at me, making a shooing motion.

Mar leads me to the dance area, where some slow Spanish music I don't recognise is playing.

"There!" Mar breathes in satisfaction. "Sometimes it's nice to get away from all the noise and chatter!"

I don't point out that most of it has come from her in the first place.

"Oh no!" she says. "You can hold me properly. You aren't dancing with your grandmother!"

I cast a helpless glance in Beatriz's direction, but she is preoccupied with Iris' bib which has come loose.

She rests her head on my shoulder. "Now," she whispers. "You can tell me what you really think of Beatriz."

I laugh. "I haven't told her, so I probably shouldn't start by telling you."

She looks at me with dark slow eyes. "You don't have to, anyway. I can tell—you like her a lot, don't you?"

I try and shrug, which is not that practical when you are dancing with someone.

"Take some advice from an old married woman. You don't get many chances to be happy. Beatriz and I, we were at university together, we've been friends ever since. I never knew anyone who was sweeter and kinder. Don't let her get away!"

I don't need to get drawn into this. Mar is, at least, tipsy. "I've only known her since February."

She smiles up into my face. "When you know, you know. And see how good she is with the children!"

This is getting very weird, very fast. I've never liked anyone telling me what to do or burrowing into my private life. Neither am I remotely keen on weans. There's something warm and genuine about Mar, though, and her affection for her friend is so obvious, that I forgive her telling me that Beatriz should be having my babies. Here, in this fairytale castle, nothing is real. Tomorrow it will be only a bewitched dream.

Soon after our dance, Mar and Artur make their excuses. Felip has become overtired and fractious, and even Beatriz cannot soothe him.

"It was so lovely to meet you, Tomàs!" cries Mar, clinging to me. "I hope so much that we see you again, and soon!"

Artur contents himself with a grin and a handshake. "See you again, perhaps."

Gathering their children and all their bags and toys, they

take themselves off down the steps. I feel a strange pang at their departure.

"What?" says Beatriz, looking at me.

I laugh and shake my head. "I don't know. You have nice friends, that's all."

She beams. "I'm glad you like them. Mar can be, you know—"

"I noticed."

The sun is long gone, and Beatriz and I are standing on the castle battlements. The moon is only a couple of days past full and casts its light on the gently rippling sea below. No-one else is around. We could be alone in the world in our own castle. We both have glasses of cava—God knows how much we've got through, but I don't feel drunk and if Beatriz is intoxicated, it's from the surroundings and the occasion. We've come a long way from the evening with mojitos at El Gat.

"What are you thinking?" she says softly, her hand on mine.

"Me? I'm trying not to think at all. I'm just enjoying being here, now, in the moment."

Her mouth twitches into a smile. "With me?"

"I don't see anyone else."

"It has been such a wonderful day. I don't think I've ever been so happy."

"Neither have I." And it's true.

She shivers. "I should have brought a cardigan."

I put my arms round her. She looks up into my face. "I hope Mar didn't embarrass you. Everything about weddings and children. Sometimes she can be—I can't remember the English word—*entremaliat.*"

Bizarrely this is one of the Catalan words I know. "Mischievous, no? She didn't embarrass me, anyway. Everyone wants to see their friends married off. She was just a bit heavy-handed and—*borratxo*."

She laughs. "Yes, she was drunk! What did she say, while you were dancing?"

I run a finger along her collarbone. "I don't remember," I lie.

"She winked at me when she came back."

"Perhaps she had something in her eye."

"Perhaps."

She pauses and leans into me. I can't see her expression. "You know, when I get married, I don't care if it's in a castle. All that matters is the person you are marrying."

I'm not sure why she's telling me this. Do I want to find out?

"Although," she continues. "A castle is pretty cool."

I laugh. "Yes. A castle certainly is cool."

You don't start this kind of conversation unless you have a destination in mind, do you? Mar might be *entremaliat* and playful, but Beatriz isn't—not about this sort of thing, anyway.

Something flippant and cynical springs to my lips, to take the emotion out of the situation, but I don't say it. In the moment, I'm overcome by the moonlight, the sea, the castle, the soft warmth of Beatriz against me, the tang of the cava drifting up from her glass.

She senses it, and twists to look me. She reaches up to kiss me. "Don't say anything," she says, trembling. "Don't say anything."

I don't know what she wants, and I don't know what I want either. But if it involves Beatriz, with or without a castle, I'm in. Whatever I might have said if I'd had the chance, there'll always be tomorrow.

PART FIVE
8 JUNE—5 AUGUST 2014

ANYONE BUT ME

I

The only thing I remember about studying *Anna Karenina* at university is the famous quote "All happy families are alike, but every unhappy family is unhappy in its own way". The same goes for relationships, I guess, because the time Beatriz and I are happiest is the part where I have nothing interesting to say.

And it's the little moments you remember afterwards. Slow-dancing to Mazzy Star in her flat. Her hand outstretched trying to coax a reluctant cat down from a wall. The look on her face when Montse climbs on the table at Broadway to sing an obscene Republican song from the civil war. Both of us singing along to "A Perfect Day to Chase Tornados" in a thunderstorm on the motorway to Tarragona. For what it's worth, I appreciate those moments at the time. Every last second.

We spend a lot of time together, of course, and although she can be prickly and insecure at times, the next few months are idyllic. After Castell de Claramunt, although neither of us says anything about the future of our relationship, it takes on an extra solidity and permanence. If the madness of nearly proposing to her on the castle walls has passed, the emotions underlying it—for both of us—have not. We take another trip, this time to Sitges, in her knackered red Seat: a swish seaside resort, crowded and noisy when I'd gone the previous August, but cool and relaxed in early June this time around. Perfect weather, perfect harmony. For those brief days I know nothing can touch us. The sun is shining, and we fit together like jigsaw pieces.

As we lounge on the golden beach, I take dozens of snaps on my phone of her posing in her bikini, and Hannah fleetingly crosses my mind. I'd sent her a brief note severing our connection in March, and the fact that she hasn't responded, even to ask for the money back, confirms my assumption that there are no Russians. She can't touch me. So far from being part of a grand heist, she's in fact managed to con herself out of ten thousand euros, now sitting in a separate bank account in my name. If this was a novel, there'd be a horrific reckoning round the corner. But this is real life and, just this once, I'm going to come out ahead.

Late in July, Beatriz and I spend another weekend in Sitges. This proves to be a mistake: by now the resort is getting crowded with cranky exiles from Barcelona, and Beatriz is tetchy throughout. We don't exactly argue—her aggression when she shows it was of the passive kind—but I might prefer that to pouting and monosyllables. I don't know what I might have done wrong, but I think we're both disappointed that Sitges has not provided the same raptures as our first visit.

The traffic back into Barcelona on the Sunday night is grinding stop-start, and at the best of times Beatriz is an impatient and erratic driver. By the time she's dropped me at my flat, parking in the extortionate adjoining car park, it's gone midnight and she decides it's not worth driving back to Carrer del Tigre. So she stays in my flat, which is unusual as hers is both bigger and smarter. This would normally be a treat but tonight I'd be happy to see the back of her.

I have a decent bottle of wine—Hannah's money and Beatriz's taste have improved most aspects of my life—and as we're both too wired from the drive to go to sleep, we sit and drank it in bed.

I don't want to fight with her. "Is everything OK, Triz?"

She takes my hand and looks at me with sad eyes. "Sorry. I've been a real bitch this weekend."

"Well..."

She laughs briefly. "You know when things are going well, you expect everything to go wrong?"

"Sometimes they don't though." Although I've had this feeling since the moment I met her, with better reason.

She snuggles into my chest so I can't see her face. I stroke her hair as she says: "You and me. Everything has been so good, hasn't it?"

This is safer ground. I've got used to lulling her insecurities. "Of course. You have to enjoy the moment."

She rolls over to look at me. "It's been so intense, though, you know? It just makes me feel so tired sometimes, worrying about what might happen."

"Ssshhh. It's OK."

Her eyes are brimming. She sits up and hugs her knees to her. "I don't mean to be like this. You will get fed up with me. It's just—I can't explain how I feel."

I pull her close to me. These melancholic fits normally cry themselves out. "I'm not fed up with you, Triz. You are the best thing that's ever happened to me." And the worst, but we won't go there.

I hold her until her sobs subside and she's asleep.

2

The next morning it's as if it never happened. We share a couple of stale croissants for breakfast, and black coffee as I don't have any milk.

She's dressed for work from the small wardrobe she maintains at my place, putting on mascara in the tiny mirror by the window.

"What are you going to do today?" she says.

"I'm sending the first chapters to Polly." Since we've been together I've been able to make some progress on the new book. Polly is some way short of delighted that I'm writing a fantasy novel—it's too downmarket for Kilpatrick & Robinson, for a start—but I've told her I think it's good and she's grudgingly agreed to see what she can do with it.

She beams. "Tomàs! I love it when you are writing." She takes personal credit for my new productivity, which is fair enough. She's created some spectacular pieces of her own over the past couple of months too.

. . .

No-one, as they say, expects the Spanish Inquisition, and in this case the quip is almost literally correct.

As she's getting ready to go, there's a knock at the door. It's not even nine o'clock, so I pull the chain and open it carefully.

A man of about forty-five with a scruffy moustache in a shabby brown suit, beige shirt and plain tie stands in front of me. "Senyor Thomas Chisholm?"

"That's me."

He pulls out a laminated card. "Inspector Rosell. Mossos d'Esquadra, Criminal Investigation Division." The Catalan police. "May I come in?"

"Tomàs! Who is it?" calls Beatriz from the kitchen area.

"The police," I say in a numb voice. I don't know why he's here but I hardly have a clear conscience.

I step aside from the door to let him in.

"You will prefer we speak English?" he says in my language.

"I'm not good with Catalan," I say, "but Spanish will be fine."

"*Bueno*. But let me practice my English."

I motion him to sit down, and he takes the sofa, which leaves nowhere for Beatriz or me unless we want to be in uncomfortable proximity to him.

"You are a British national, but resident in Barcelona?"

"That's correct," I say. "I have a lease on this flat, I've lived here for two and a half years."

"And your occupation?"

"I teach English to Spanish students, and I'm a writer."

Rosell pulls out a pen and notebook and jots a sentence or two. "These are well-paid professions?"

"Not especially," I snap. "As I'm sure you know. Look, what is this about?" I feel a rare urge for a cigarette.

"Please, senyor," he says. "I have some questions, not many, but it will be quicker and easier if you let me ask them."

Beatriz rests a trembling hand on my forearm. I can smell the light sweetness of her perfume.

"You will not think me impolite if I ask how you live?" he continues.

"It is not exactly a friendly question." I point to the copies of *Fear and Loathing in Kilmarnock* on the shelves. "If you must know, I wrote a book in Britain, and my publisher has paid me to write another one."

Rosell nods, and in his drab suit and hangdog manner he reminds me of Peter Falk as Columbo. A detective who feigns stupidity and always gets his man. If it wasn't August in Barcelona, I know he'd be wearing a mac.

"Where were you, please, between eight and ten p.m. on Thursday evening?"

Home alone, while Beatriz was consoling Estel over some dating calamity. But not doing anything criminal, at least.

"With me," says Beatriz. "We were in my flat in the Raval all evening."

I look at her from the corner of my eye. Never a bad thing to have an alibi if the polis are asking, but still.

"Senyoreta? You are?" Rosell cocks an inquisitive head.

"Beatriz Bernat. I'm Tommy's girlfriend."

"You can imagine, Senyoreta Bernat, that an alibi from a girlfriend is not always conclusive."

She shrugs. "That's where we were. I'm sorry we didn't have hundreds of witnesses."

"You still haven't told us what this is about," I say.

He lifts a hand. "There was a serious assault on Thursday evening," he says. "A man, in the hospital, unconscious. Maybe forever."

I lick my lips. Whatever I might be guilty of, it's not this. For some reason that makes me feel even shiftier.

"A Senyor—" he consults his notebook, which is clearly a sham "—Senyor Ignacio Fuentes."

"Ignacio?" This is senseless.

"You know Senyor Fuentes?"

"Slightly. We have a drink occasionally, go the football."

"Senyoreta? You know this man?"

"I've never heard of him," she says through tight lips.

"I don't think Beatriz has ever met him," I say.

Rosell smiles. "Ah, different social circles, eh? Perhaps I am old-fashioned, maybe these days they say sexist, but Senyoreta Bernat, a woman of class and distinction, no?"

"And?"

"Senyor Fuentes, perhaps not so much."

"I barely know the man, Inspector. I was with Beatriz when the—assault—happened. I'm sorry that something has happened to Ignacio, but I don't understand why you're here."

It's easiest for now to go along with her false alibi. I can hardly call her a liar in front of Rosell.

Beatriz looks across at me. "You'll be late for work," I say. "You can go while I sort this out with Inspector Rosell."

She sets her mouth, digs her hands into her jeans pockets. "I'm not going anywhere."

Rosell flips through his notebook. "You say you know Senyor Fuentes 'slightly'? You are on good terms, yes?"

I shrug. "You like football, Inspector? That's all we talk about, and surely that's true of most men. It's cool to support Espanyol rather than Barça, no?"

Rosell grunts. "When did you last see him?"

"Not for a couple of months. New girlfriend, you know. The last time we went out he thought Levante's goal was offside and I didn't, but that's hardly..."

A nod. "Can you explain why a Senyoreta—" he flips

theatrically through his notebook again "—Senyoreta Carmen Cerda said that you had quarrelled? She says Senyor Fuentes was much upset."

Fuck. The Ashtray.

I glance sideways at Beatriz, who is regarding me with a cool inspection, her mouth pursed like a cat's arse.

I say carefully: "Carmen and I dated for a few weeks. She doesn't like me, and I imagine she'd say anything to get me in trouble."

Rosell scratches at his moustache. "So the young lady is lying?"

I shrug. "She wasn't there. So let's say mistaken."

"When did you last see the senyoreta?"

"Carmen? I haven't kept count. It was a pretty casual relationship. I don't know, January?"

"A casual relationship, a casual friendship. You don't seem to be very attached to anyone."

I look at Beatriz, whose expression is unreadable.

"Sure I am. Just not those two."

A smile creeps over his face. "And Senyoreta Bernat?"

"I've already told you. She's my girlfriend. So yes, I'm attached to her."

"And Senyoreta Cerda, she was your girlfriend too?"

"No!" This comes out more vehemently than I'd intended. "We went out a few times."

Rosell holds up a placating hand. "It's so difficult to tell with young people. Facebook, Tinder... I don't know how you stay on top of it all."

He may dress like Columbo but I doubt he's more than ten years older than me. The curmudgeon act is just that. I walk to the door and open it.

"Do you have any more questions, Inspector? I don't know

anything about what happened to Ignacio, I was with Beatriz when it happened, and Carmen is a lying shrew with a grudge."

"My apologies for taking up your time, Senyor Chisholm. That's all. For today. I may need to ask you some more questions later." He chuckles. "'Don't leave town', I think they say. I can see myself out."

3

I SHUT THE DOOR WITH A SOFT ANGRY INTENSITY. BEATRIZ IS simmering.

"What the fuck was that Tomàs?" She can swear in English but she almost never does when she's sober.

"Go to work, Triz. We'll talk about it tonight." I need some time to get my head clear.

"We will talk about it now," she hisses. "Who are these people? You were lying to the detective."

"Only to cover the false alibi you gave me. Which I didn't need. Because I haven't done anything."

"'*Gràcies*, Beatriz, for lying to the police for me'." Her tone is the staccato monotone she usually saves for Catalan. "I might have known you wouldn't appreciate it."

I sit down heavily on the sofa. "Of course I appreciate it, B. It's just you didn't have to."

"You don't know the police here. He might smile, he might be polite, but if he suspects you, believe me, you need an alibi."

I stand up, put my hands on her shoulders. I can feel her shaking. "It'll sort itself out. Trust me."

She shrugs me off. "So why does he come here? Why does he think you would hurt this—Ignacio?"

I attempt an easy smile. "I've known Ignacio a year or so, we've been to a couple of Espanyol games together. I don't know him that well."

She points at the Espanyol crest tattooed on her ankle. "You know I go to watch Espanyol, but you've never mentioned him?"

She's keeping her voice level with an effort, and I wish she'd just let go. I don't understand why she's raging.

"I don't tell you every tiny detail about my life, B."

Her cheeks are flushed and there's a fleck of spittle at the corner of her mouth. "No, Tomàs, it doesn't look like you do. You didn't tell me about—" she spits the word out "—Carmen."

"Come on, B, that was before I even knew you!"

"And she meant nothing to you." Her voice was ominously quiet.

"Of course not."

"And when will you say that about me? When you are with someone else?"

We've kind of been here before, although not with this viciousness. She has insecurities which I know I will always have to manage somehow. I can usually talk her down from this. So why the fuck do I say what I do next?

"Like you told me about Jaume?"

I don't give a fuck about Jaume. He's a pitiful loser, a guy who preys on and exploits women. I've said it to wound, not to win the argument.

She pales. "Who told you about that?"

"Not you, which is all that matters." Bizarrely I feel an obligation to keep Aleix out of trouble. "So I should have told you about Carmen, who you've never even heard of, but you don't think to mention you had a crush on Jaume for a year and then you went out with him?"

"Did Estel tell you that? I will scratch her eyes out." Still her voice hasn't risen above a growl. "I made a mistake with Jaume, and I was embarrassed, Tommy, embarrassed! Can you understand that? I didn't want you to think I was so stupid."

I feel sick. "Triz..."

"And you talk about Carmen as if she's rubbish, some slut off the street. So it's not the same at all. If you think about her like that, how do you think about me?"

I can't win here. Carmen was a clatty bitch but if I disparage her, Beatriz will think I'd do the same about her, and if I don't she'll think I don't care about her.

I sigh. "Beatriz, can't we talk about this later?"

"The police were here! We need to talk about it now."

"No we don't." I try and put an edge of menace in my voice, because the whole thing will unravel if we end up here.

"So what I want to talk about doesn't matter, hey?" Her voice is barely audible. "I thought you were different."

This whole thing has hit bang on her fault line—her inability to trust men, lack of confidence and self-esteem, her worries that our relationship was always on the verge of imminent collapse. How much of her rigid self-control is natural and how much is that she's scared? Scared of saying the wrong thing, scared of upsetting people, scared of losing what's important to her?

And I've done this to her. Who am I kidding? I'm no better than Jaume. Worse, if anything.

I move towards her but she pushes past me to the door. "I thought you were different, Tommy," she repeats. "I thought you were different."

She slams the door behind her and as she clatters down the stairs in her work heels I can hear her howl in rage and pain.

. . .

I lock the door behind me and try to corral my thoughts into what I'm going to say to Rosell about Ignacio. When I think of Beatriz my mind screams like a stripped gear but I can’t think about anything else.

4

I LIE ON MY BED, AND BEFORE I KNOW IT, THE AFTERNOON IS HERE. THE fridge is empty and I drag myself to get some lunch and stock up at the supermarket. It looks like I'm going to be eating by myself for a while.

By July, the temperature in Barcelona is unbearable, especially for a Scot. I might have Hannah's money to tide me over, but the city which has delighted me for the past two years feels as oppressive as the heat, and the next couple of months aren't going to get any better. The language classes have wound up for the summer, so I don't even have that to keep me occupied.

I sit outside a café and have an omelette with a beer. The chair and table are cheap aluminium and the light pierces my eyes even through my RayBans. I used to love just sitting outside, watching people and lapping up the city. But now, having spent so much time with Beatriz and the rest, I don't know what to do with myself. The real Barcelona isn't the architecture or the climate, it's the people.

I wish I had a cigarette, but I can't be bothered to get up and put the five euros in the machine. Instead I signal for another beer. I can't keep my mind away from Beatriz anymore. Her sudden anger surprised me, and as far as Carmen went it's complete overreaction, but her underlying grievance, that I don't trust her enough to share everything with her, is right enough. She needs to be with someone open and trustworthy. That hadn't been Jaume and, I can't deny, it's not me either. Is she attracted to men who'll break her heart? I'm hardly qualified on the subject, but perhaps she needs therapy. When I'd broken up with Carmen, she'd shrugged, called me a son of a bitch (although in Catalan, *fill de puta* is so much more musical) and lit a cigarette. It would have been so much easier if Beatriz had just called me a *fill de puta*. Although if what Rosell said was true, Carmen has decided revenge is a dish best served cold.

Beatriz is better off without me. She's talented, has the sweetest disposition underneath the angst, loving and generous. She needs someone like Aleix, if he wasn't gay. I smirk at the thought and take another pull at my beer.

My phone rings on the table next to my empty plate. Who the fuck uses a phone for conversation these days? Unless it's Beatriz? I glance down at the display. Hannah. For fuck's sake! She's the last person I want to speak to, and I click abruptly to decline the call. We've had no contact since March, and that's fine with me. Seconds later a text comes through: pick up the fucking phone. This removes any doubt that someone else might be using her phone. The message is pure Hannah.

It buzzes again. I watch it for three rings and then answer.

"Aye?"

"We need to speak, Chisholm."

"Fuck off, Hannah. We're done, remember? And since when did we talk on the phone?"

"These aren't normal times, are they? You heard about Ignacio?"

Christ, it's all going to shite again. "Yes, I heard about Ignacio."

"That's why we need to meet, and I don't want a trail of texts. Now where the fuck are you?"

There's no way out of this. I need to know what she knows, and what she wants. "You come to me," I say. "I'm ten minutes from your office and I'm settled in for a session." I give her the address.

In all the drama with Beatriz, it's only now occurred to me to question my certainty that the Russians were imaginary. But someone has beaten up Ignacio. It could be coincidence, an unfortunate mischance, but equally the violent organised criminals whose existence I've so breezily discounted might be on the scene after all. It's time to hear what Hannah has to say.

Fifteen minutes later she appears at my table, looking like an office worker who's slipped out for a late lunch, kitten heels, charcoal pencil skirt, white blouse and a Celine tote bag. She fishes out a packet of cigarettes and lights one, calling to the waiter for a coffee.

She blows the smoke into my face. "Long time, no see, eh?"

"Not long enough."

"I had a boyfriend once," she says, leaning back on the uncomfortable aluminium chair and crossing her legs.

"I didn't realise we were doing show and tell."

"We went fishing off the Gulf of Mexico, hired a fuck-off motorboat and a skipper."

"Don't tell me. The boyfriend ended up at the bottom of the sea and you shagged the skipper."

She ignores me. "The most boring two days of my life."

"And you a lawyer? Wow. That's saying something."

"Eventually Gary caught a fish, I can't even remember what it was, a marlin or a swordfish or some big fucker. It took three hours to land."

"I've read *The Old Man and the Sea*, and I didn't reckon much to it. This is no more interesting. Just get to the fucking point."

"Shit, chill out, Chisholm. This is the 'fucking point': for that whole three hours, the fish had a hook in its mouth. It ran the line out and it thought it was free. But it wasn't free at all. It was dead and it just didn't know it yet."

I say nothing.

"You read literature so you understand metaphors and shit, but I'll spell it out anyway. You're the fish, Chisholm. You're the fucking fish."

My fingers twitch. "Give me a cigarette."

She raises an eyebrow, lights one and passes it over.

"The hook was there all the time," she says. "Now the Russians are reeling you in. It's showtime."

I'm glad I still have my sunglasses on so she can't read my eyes. "What part of my resignation letter did you not understand?"

She laughs and shakes her head. "Do you think the Russians have a fucking HR department? You're in bollock-deep until they say you're out."

"I thought you wanted to talk to me about Ignacio. The police showed up on my doorstep this morning. They think I did it."

She chuckles. "Well, I believe in your innocence."

"I have an alibi." She's not to know it's shite.

"And of course it was the Russians. They didn't have to go quite that far, but they are not happy. Not happy at all."

"But I got the impression that Ignacio worked for them." Now that it seems they're real after all.

"They're sending a message, Chisholm. And the message is for you."

"I don't speak crook."

"I'd hoped you'd be a bit more perceptive, what with you

being a writer." She stubs her cigarette out, then lights another one. I've never understood why people do that.

"The Russians need you, for now. They can't hurt you, and they can't hurt your little friends in case they run. But Ignacio is theirs, bought and paid for."

"And what about you? Do they kick the shite out of you if this goes tits up?"

She smiles and sips her coffee. "I think I can be pretty effective at shifting the blame onto you, Chisholm."

I sigh and call for another beer. None of this is really a surprise. "It's not that straightforward. I've split up with Beatriz, so I can't use her, and the others won't help me without her."

Hannah shakes her head ruefully. "And you're so charming, Chisholm! I don't understand women sometimes."

I flick my cigarette butt into the street in a sudden burst of annoyance. "We were getting on just fine until the polis showed up," I snap. "So maybe your gangster masterminds beating up Ignacio wasn't the best idea, eh? Because then I wouldn't have had to deal with fucking Columbo knocking on my door."

"I'll tell them that, shall I? Look, you've had a tiff, just kiss and make up. Do I have to tell you how to do this? Buy her some flowers, spend some of the money I gave you to take her to dinner at Dos Cielos, then fuck her brains out. Tomorrow it's like it never happened. It's not that difficult."

I whip my sunglasses off and bite down on the urge to slap her. "You are—"

She grins at me and leans forward. "What am I, Chisholm?" she says in a low voice.

"You are...repulsive." Somewhere I feel like I'm striking a tiny blow for Beatriz.

She laughs so loudly the couple at the next table look over. She reaches into her bag and slips a cheap-looking Alcatel phone across to me. “Eventually the police may want to look at your phone,” she says. “So don’t contact me on it. Use this one to text me for meetings, nothing else. Got it?” I nod. “It doesn’t come with a charger, but I'm trusting you to sort that out yourself. You’ve got a week to make some progress.”

She gets up and throws down a couple of euros for the coffee. “I’ve missed you, Chisholm,” she says as she turns and walks away.

I watch her as she merges into the crowd. *You’ve got your fucking fish, Hannah.*

I go back to the flat on Catfish Alley and crash down on the bed. I knew this moment was coming, the same way I knew Beatriz and I would end in flames. But I’ve sleepwalked into both of those situations anyway. It doesn’t say much for my intelligence or my vigour. When I was younger, I loved Robert Goddard’s thrillers, inevitably involving an ordinary man, drawn into events outside his control, and working his way free through cunning, ingenuity and pluck. I know for certain now that I’m no Robert Goddard hero: I can do ‘ordinary’ in spades but otherwise I’m waiting for the inevitable. It’s time, appropriately enough in this country, to take the bull by the horns.

A few weeks ago the aircon in the building broke down and the landlord had called out engineers to repair the unit on the roof. I hadn’t realised before that you could get up there, and since then I’ve started using it as an improvised roof terrace, a couple of upturned packing crates serving as table and chair. The guy on the floor above me, Carles, who might have had a claim on it by proximity, doesn’t seem interested. I hardly know him, a single man in his sixties slouching around in a grubby white vest and a beer gut. From time to time he offers me a chilling glimpse into my own future.

Now I go up onto the roof although, even in the shade of the aircon units, it's too hot for comfort. I can't take the room anymore, though, and neither can I face another bar or café. I sip at a bottle of water from the fridge as I sit on the crate and look out over the city. The heat has burned all the uncertainty away. I only have two options. Get back into bed with Beatriz, literally if I'm lucky, or run. Staying here and waiting for the Russians to get even more pissed off with me, until they beat me half to death like Ignacio, is the worst of all worlds.

Looked at that way, the fight with Beatriz has probably helped. It's not like I have the temptation to stay here and try to make it work with her anymore. She's better off without me, even I can't deny that, and the best thing I can do for her is leave her be. She'll be hurt—why kid myself, maybe even heart-broken—but once she gets over it, she'll be free and clear. In a week she and Estel will be giving my name dog's abuse over mojitos, and in six months they'll be saying 'who was that *fill de puta* again?' And maybe, given her taste in men, by then Beatriz will have found some other manipulative shit to cut her to pieces, but that won't be my problem. *Adéu,* Beatriz.

There's moisture on my cheeks and I hope it's sweat. I press the cool water bottle against my face.

So it's run, then. I should have known from the start. I can start somewhere else in Europe, but the money won't last long and if it's not Spain I won't speak the language. Or I could go up into the mountains—rent a run-down old cottage in the Alpujarras for a few thousand euros a year—and wait for the heat to die down. Exile, country air, just me and the mountains, and a novel to write. And that's just fine—*bé,* as the Catalans put it—except that I'd have so much time with my own thoughts. Up there, penned in by a cold damp winter, I reckon the inside of my head might end up doing me more harm than the Russians.

Shit. So it has to be Kilmarnock. The place holds almost no memories I want to revisit, Gillian will tear the hide off me the way only a big sister can, and the last time I saw Dad I'd told him I'd put my fist through his face if I ever saw him again. Aye, those relationships could be better. And my old room in the grim terrace I grew up in, Mum fifteen years in her grave... But if I need six months or a year to get myself back on my feet, save some money and decide what next, Kilmarnock is probably the only place to do it. It's not an ideal writing environment, but the fantasy novel is coming along quickly enough and I ought to be able to get a first draft to Polly by Christmas.

I sigh and drain my water bottle, wipe my forehead and slouch back downstairs to the flat where the laptop and the Expedia website are waiting.

My resolution lasts for as long as it takes me to check prices—how much!—and I decide this isn't a decision to make on the spur of the moment. Hannah told me I had a week to come back to her, so I can string her along for seven days at least, maybe a bit more. Kilmarnock will fall into the pit of hell at some point, but probably not over the next week. It'll still be there if I need it.

5

I HAVEN'T SEEN IGNACIO SINCE WE QUARRELLED IN MARCH, AND I'VE not got much to thank him for. He's the one who introduced me to Carmen and Hannah and look how they turned out. But I don't like to think of him lying half-dead in the hospital. I've no reason to believe what Rosell's told me about his condition, though, and all in all it might be a good idea to pay him a visit. I don't know how seriously Rosell suspects me, or the weight he's giving Carmen's innuendoes, but I know I'm innocent. It can't do any harm to take him some chocolates (I imagine fags and beer are out, and I can't see him eating grapes).

Before I can talk myself out of it, I hop on the metro. I know where the hospital is because it's literally across the road from Broadway. I stop off at the Bonpreu supermarket to pick up a gift, ending up with a box of Ferrero Rocher, the universal choice for when you don't really know what to get someone, and make my way up to the hospital.

The foyer is clean and impersonal, and this extends to the receptionists too.

"You are the family of Senyor Fuentes?"

So he's here, at least, and I'd already anticipated the question.

"Yes. I'm his cousin."

The receptionist—a badge on her blouse says María Teresa—peers at me suspiciously over her half-moon glasses.

"You are English."

"Actually I'm—yes, I'm English. My mother is his aunt."

They can't possibly check this, surely.

María Teresa ponders for a moment, then nods. "Take that lift, two floors, left, Santa Cruz Ward."

That was easy enough. I thank her and take the lift. The new corridor has no windows, and fluorescent lights create an endless artificial day. My trainers squeak on the tiled floor as I walk towards the ward reception, and I go through the cousin routine again, this time with "Pepe".

"Senyor Fuentes is not able to have visitors. He is sedated."

"Can someone tell me how he is?"

"One moment," says Pepe, picking up her phone and pushing a button. "You wait over there, please?" She indicated a bank of empty plastic seats.

A minute later a figure in a navy-blue Mossos uniform appears. No name-badge here. It should have occurred to me that Ignacio would have a police guard. "Senyor Chisholm?"

I stand up so at least we're on a level. "That's right."

"The cousin of Senyor Fuentes?"

Hmmm. Let's not get into the habit of lying to the cops.

"More of a friend, actually. But I'm sure he'd like to see me."

"You know he was attacked, yes? Very sick."

"That's why I came."

"He cannot have visitors. Only family, with police supervision."

I'm beginning to wonder why I came. I know that Ignacio is

really here, and that he's badly injured—all of which I already knew if I'd not tried to second-guess Rosell.

"Sorry to have bothered you, pal." I hold out the Ferrero Rocher. "Perhaps you could..."

He makes no effort to take the chocolates, and I drop my arm limply back to my side.

There's a clacking of heels on the lino and a shriek. "*Què fa aquí!*" What is he doing here?

Shit. Good question. I really should have thought of this as well.

"Hello, Carmen," I say as neutrally as I can.

She stands in front of me, her low heels bringing her eyes level with mine. "You attack him and then you show up here."

She turns to the cop. "I told Inspector Rosell, this man quarrelled with Ignacio. He should have been arrested!"

The cop takes a step back. Carmen in full flow is best negotiated from a distance. "I will report that he was here. If Inspector Rosell had wanted to arrest him, he would have done."

Carmen purses her lips.

"Be reasonable," I say to her. This is a mistake.

"Reasonable! Ignacio is in intensive care! I told the police that you had a fight with him, you should not be anywhere near him now!"

"It wasn't a fight—"

Her hands tighten around the cigarette packet she's holding.

"Come on," I say. "Let's talk outside." She may be less aggressive with some nicotine in her lungs.

She shrugs. "I'm going out anyway."

The cop is on his radio so I probably don't want to hang around here longer than I have to anyway. Carmen and I get into the lift in silence. As we step out onto the street she puts on a pair of big round sunglasses that cover up her expression.

"You've lost weight," I say as she lights her cigarette. She was always slim, but in skinny jeans, a tight t-shirt and her hair scraped back from her face, she looks skeletal now.

She shakes her head in baffled disgust. "Maybe being at the hospital twenty hours a day, you don't get much chance to eat."

"They say you can never be too thin, right?"

She pushes her sunglasses up into her hair to give me the full force of her glare. "What are you doing here? You haven't spoken to Ignacio for months."

I look down at the pavement. "You can't really believe I'd hurt him, Carmen."

She shrugs. "He said you had quarrelled, really quarrelled. He wouldn't say why."

"And the idea of getting me in trouble with the police had nothing to do with what you said to Rosell?"

She takes a drag on her cigarette. "I don't think about you from one month to the next. The police asked me if Ignacio had any enemies, I told them about your fight. End of."

"It's not fucking 'end of', though, is it? Not for me. It's just the fucking start."

She gave me a bleak smile. "The police asked me a question. I answered it."

"Apparently Ignacio has a criminal record. You don't think there are other people more likely to give him a kicking?"

She shrugs again. What had I ever seen in her?

"The police showed up my flat," I say. "My girlfriend was there."

There's an expression in her eyes I can't read.

"She was so horrified by it all that she dumped me."

"I'm sorry about that." She laughs. "Did you ever hear of karma?"

I take her wrist as she's lifting her cigarette to her lips. "Carmen, do you really want revenge so badly you'd set the police on me? What we had, it wasn't that big a deal."

She snatches her hand free. "You think this is all about you, Tommy? I really don't give a fuck about you. I want Ignacio to wake up, and I want whoever hurt him to be caught."

"And you think that's me?" I ask softly. "That's really what you think of me?"

She holds my gaze. "No. But I never knew you, Tommy. I never knew you at all."

She stubs her cigarette out on the wall and walks back towards the entrance. She looks back over her shoulder. "Don't come here again."

PART SIX
11—12 AUGUST 2014

A PERFECT DAY TO CHASE TORNADOS§

I

I WISH I COULD SAY I USED THE NEXT FEW DAYS TO SAY A MELANCHOLY farewell to the city where I'd been happy, by and large, for the past couple of years. In fact, other than a trip to the supermarket, I don't go out of the flat, trying to read Raymond Chandler on the roof terrace in the cool mornings and evenings. When it gets too hot in the middle of the day, I slump in my chair in the apartment, the laptop power light winking insolently at me, daring me to open it and book my flight.

I desperately want to text Beatriz, if only to say goodbye. I don't have the strength to do it, and text is brutal and impersonal anyway. Leave her to hate me.

I'm resigned to it ending, a grim anti-climax and a bitter tactical retreat, when Aleix gets in contact.

Heard about u and btrz. Sorry to hear it. wanna meet up for a drink?

Thanx but no thanx

Broadway tonite 8-30. Guarantee the others not there.

And really, what else have I got to do? It's my chance, indirectly, to say goodbye to the whole group, because Aleix isn't known for his discretion.

Ok. Bé.

I'm surprised at the pang of nostalgia I feel as I walk through the door at Broadway. It's only a couple of weeks since I was last there, and I've always liked the vibe, but the world has changed. My world, anyway. Broadway seems not to have noticed.

Aleix is there, dressed in what passes for smart casual with him: a maroon waistcoat, a tie from a designer that Beatriz would have recognised, crisp white shirt, razor-edged charcoal slacks and black patent leather brogues. He shakes my hand with an expression more consistent with recent bereavement, and we sit at a table in the corner on the upper floor. It's a table Beatriz and I had once used, but he's not to know that.

"*Com estàs*? How are you?" he asks.

I shrug. "I've been better."

Aleix orders two Martinis and I sip mine with distaste. It's not a drink I ever cared for.

"I'm really sorry you guys broke up."

I look at him over the lip of my glass. "The only time we

talked about this before, you warned me off her and said we weren't good for each other."

Aleix gives an embarrassed half-smile. "Well, that part was right. But she was happy with you, you know? Maybe I was wrong."

"History now, isn't it?"

He claps my arm. "Don't be like that. We don't know each other that well, but I think you were happy too."

"It's irrelevant. The better it was then, the worse it makes it now."

"Listen," he says, playing with the olive in his glass. "I've broken up with a lot of guys in my time."

I almost smile. "You surprise me."

"Most of the time, good riddance to bad rubbish." He makes a brushing motion with his hands. "But sometimes you think, oh, he was nice!"

"Best not to do regrets, pal."

"What do I know? But I thought you and Beatriz had something."

My mind flashes back to the wedding in Tarragona, the castle battlements under the moonlight.

His phone rings in his jacket pocket. He pulls it out, his wallet falling to the floor as he does so. I reach down to pick it up, but he snatches it out of my hand before I can give it back, muttering into the phone in rapid Catalan. "I'll call you back," he finishes, stuffing his wallet back into his pocket.

"Sorry about that," he says. "Work, you know."

"Not me. I work for myself."

His expression suggests he knows how elastic my idea of work is.

"What we were saying before—Estel thinks you and Beatriz were good together too," he says.

"Jesus, Aleix, is this the fucking gossip of Barcelona?"

He raises his palms and chuckles. "Estel and I talk."

"Just you and Estel?"

He grins. "We've not had a conversation with Beatriz if that's what you mean. Wouldn't dare if I'm honest. Ask her how she is, she just snaps 'OK'."

"*Bé*," I say, biting it down to a half-syllable the way she does when she's in queen of passive aggression mode.

"*Bé*," he laughs. "Just like that."

He pauses and shakes his head. "Call me a sentimental old romantic," he says. "But you loved each other. And you still do."

"For God's sake, Aleix!" Heads turn in the bar. "I've known her since February. We had a thing, like you do sometimes, and now it's over."

Aleix makes to say something. I cut him off. "I'm leaving Barcelona, anyway. So none of it matters."

He raises both eyebrows. "Leaving? Does she know?"

"No. I only decided this week."

"Because of her?"

"Not everything is about this tragic passionate love affair you want to make it, Aleix."

"Can I tell her? And Estel?"

I shrug. "It's not a secret."

2

It's as well that I haven't booked a flight out because the next day Inspector Rosell calls asking me to attend the police station for a formal interview. I ask if I can bring a lawyer and he says that this would be 'advisable'. So we put it off until the day after tomorrow to give me time to get in contact with Hannah, who, like it or not, is going to share this ordeal.

As I'd expected, she's unenthusiastic.

"Do you think I want to get dragged into this, Chisholm?" she snaps as we take our seats at Cafè Viena. "I've set up a burner phone for a reason."

"Join the fucking gang, Hannah. I didn't ask for this either. Rosell told me to bring a lawyer. And since I'm not normally on the wrong side of the law, I don't know many fucking lawyers," I hiss.

"Language, Chisholm," she says with a smile and a hypocrisy even I find breathtaking. "I suppose at least this way I can keep an eye on you and make sure you don't say anything you shouldn't."

She looks at me as she blows the froth on her cappuccino. "Not, of course, that you were planning to make—unwise—

revelations. You can be pretty sure the Russians have someone inside the local police."

I run a hand through my hair. "You think I'm going to drop the Russians into a polis interview? Give me credit for some sense."

Her expression suggests that, while she considered that possibility, she'd swiftly rejected it.

"Hannah—"

"—Senyora Layton—"

"For fuck's sake," I murmur. "Look, the reason I'm not going to say anything is because I'm fucking innocent. As in, didn't do it, have an alibi. Rosell is fishing because he has nothing else."

Hannah dabs foam off her lips with a napkin. "Fish, of course. And you remember the conversation we had about fish." She mimes casting a lure.

"How could I forget?"

"So, any progress in landing your own catch?"

This is the downside of arranging a meeting with her.

"You gave me a week," I say, straightening my cup in its saucer.

"Five days of which have now elapsed. I didn't expect you to leave everything to the deadline."

"I'm a fucking writer. What else did you expect?"

My phone beeps on the table in front of me—a text from Beatriz. Quickly I sweep it up and slide it into my jacket. Hannah strikes me as a woman who's used to reading things she shouldn't upside down.

"Anything interesting?" she smiles.

"If an overdraft message from your bank is interesting."

"Overdraft?" She frowns. "What happened to the money I gave you? You haven't blown it on that slut?"

I know she wants a response and I don't give it to her. "I know better than to pay ten thousand euros cash into my account," I say. "And now the polis are all over me I'm sure you're glad I didn't."

She gives this a grudging nod.

I smack my cup down with a crack of china on china. "I never wanted to be a fucking criminal at all!"

"Whoah, big boy! You were happy enough to take the money."

"Not once I knew what it was for," I say.

"Hmmm, that's what they call 'due diligence'," she says primly. "You fail to prepare; you prepare to fail."

"So I should have seen you as Senyora Scoundrel from the start?"

"Well," she says. "I would have done. A lesson for the future, maybe: if something looks too good to be true, it probably is."

"Fuck, Hannah, you're a mine of cliché this morning."

"Clichés invariably embody hard-won empirical wisdom," she says with a Mona Lisa smile. "You should maybe pay more attention."

Five minutes later she's gone, leaving me with the tab, and instructions on where to meet for our interview with Rosell.

I slip my phone back out of my pocket and order another coffee. This time I'm in the mood for a sharp black espresso. Beatriz really has sent me a text. Has Aleix spoken to her? I'd hardly encouraged him to think I'd welcome rekindling the relationship.

When we were together, we'd developed a habit of sending each other Spotify playlists. Hers, inevitably, were thoughtfully and creatively curated with artists I'd barely heard of: Echobelly, Like Spinning, Grinderman, Emma Ruth Rundle, Thievery Corporation, Jim White. There's at least a dozen songs I'll never be able to listen to again. Now she's sent me another one. A peace offering? I can almost see my heart pounding through my shirt.

I open the playlist – sixteen tracks. I run my eye down the listing: "Fuck and Run" by Liz Phair, sixteen times. OK, not a peace offering then. A passive aggressive hand-grenade. I like the song, which she knows, but its theme of women used and cast aside by men is not exactly encouraging. But at least she's talking to me, sort of.

The sensible thing to do is ignore it. I'll be gone in a week. But of course I don't—or can't, if you're being charitable. I open my own Spotify account and make a playlist of my own, just two songs, and send it back to her. "Don't Kiss Me Goodbye" by Ultra Orange and Emmanuelle and "Only Love Can Break Your Heart" by Saint Etienne. And I think how glad I am I haven't booked my flight back to Scotland.

Within a couple of minutes she's sent me a new one-song playlist. "Anyone But Me" by Josienne Clarke. I realise that first, I'll never match her for eclectic music choices and second, a song about burying in the woods a lover you don't trust is some way short of a complete reconciliation. I text her.

Maybe easier to just talk

The three dots blink on the screen while she composes her reply, which I half expect to be *Bé.* The dots disappear. Whatever she was going to say, she's reconsidered. More dots.

This isn't a good idea.

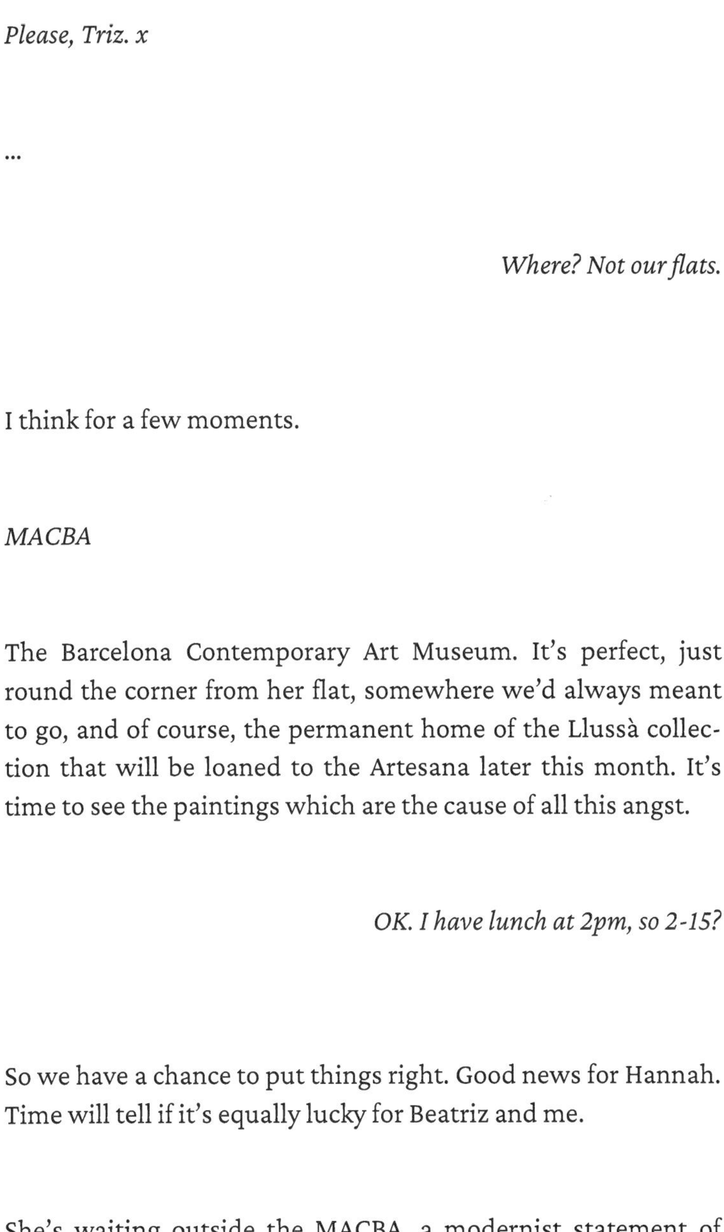

Please, Triz. x

...

Where? Not our flats.

I think for a few moments.

MACBA

The Barcelona Contemporary Art Museum. It's perfect, just round the corner from her flat, somewhere we'd always meant to go, and of course, the permanent home of the Llussà collection that will be loaned to the Artesana later this month. It's time to see the paintings which are the cause of all this angst.

OK. I have lunch at 2pm, so 2-15?

So we have a chance to put things right. Good news for Hannah. Time will tell if it's equally lucky for Beatriz and me.

She's waiting outside the MACBA, a modernist statement of glass and concrete I've never much cared for. Skateboarders are criss-crossing the paved frontage with every appearance of chaotic abandon. The sun is crushing the life out of the air, but Beatriz looks fresh, trim and composed. She's dressed in the informal style of the graphic designer she works for – black jeans and a white t-shirt, seventies-style sunglasses, hair pinned up like Audrey Hepburn. The plain black lettering on her t-shirt says *tractar amb delicadesa* – 'handle with care' and I wonder if this is a deliberate message. Her eyes are hidden behind the sunglasses and her hands are thrust nonchalantly in her back pockets. I realise how much I've missed her, and how little self-control I seem to have when I'm with her.

I make to kiss her on the cheek and she pulls me in for a hug. I break away and look into her eyes. "Triz, I'm..."

She shakes her head. "We don't have long," she says. "I need to be back at work. I already bought the tickets."

We walk into the foyer out of the sun, and she pushes her sunglasses on top of her head. I note with a suppressed amusement the real-time monitor with a video feed of the visitors, the uniformed guards around the perimeter. If this is the deterrent security, I can hardly imagine the actual measures: pressure plates, infra-red sensors, picture-specific tripwires. No wonder the Russians don't want to take the risk here. The precautions at the Artesana are amateurish in comparison. The fact that one of them is next to me, smelling of sunshine, tells me that they deserved to get robbed for sheer fucking negligence.

The MACBA turns out to be an inspired choice of venue. Beatriz, who's quiet and watchful to start with, comes alive once we're in front of the art. She has something intelligent to say about all the installations, and a couple of times she reflexively touches my hand as she points out a feature of interest. I have to say almost nothing, which in the circumstances can only be helpful.

We've been there about three-quarters of an hour and still

haven't got to wherever the Llussàs are. I don't know how soon she'll have to go back to work.

"It's on the top floor at the back," she says when I ask. "They're not exactly the most popular exhibits. Do you think they'd lend us anything they really valued?"

That's relative, I think. The collection is worth several million even if that's pocket change to the MACBA.

And so at last we find ourselves in the anteroom with about half a dozen canvasses. It's so obscure there's no-one else in the room apart from an elderly—and seemingly dozing—security guard.

"You like them?" she smiles as we glide round the room.

I screw my face up. "Not really." I can't see what they have to stimulate the Russians so much. I'm no great art historian—and the guidebook is unhelpfully pretentious wank that could have been written by Jaume—but I can make out some similarity to the Surrealist and Modernist works that everyone knows.

Llussà's signature trick seems to be transposing items within everyday scenes. There's a man walking his dog, but the man has the dog's head and vice versa. In another a bull and naked matador appear to have swapped not just heads but genitalia. The only painting I'd even heard of was *The Adoration of the Magi*, a canvas much smaller than I'd expected giving its own take on the birth of Jesus. The magi and the cattle in the stable had each other's heads, of course, and while the infant Christ had retained his own, he had a cigarette between his lips. The Virgin Mary was displaying more of her torso than was strictly necessary for breast-feeding, and Joseph had a pistol slung at one hip, a hammer and sickle on his headdress and a Catalan flag on his breast. One of the magi, despite his sheep's head, was reading a newspaper whose front page seemed to depict General Franco copulating with a goat.

My knowledge of the civil war was pretty sketchy, but I could see why none of this would have gone down a storm with the church or the Nationalists. It was little surprise that he'd been driven into exile in the mid-forties. Perhaps that explained his renewed popularity with Catalan separatists today because I couldn't see anything in the artwork that a moderately talented art student couldn't have accomplished.

Beatriz has her head on one side grinning at me. "Worth the wait?"

"I'm not sure I'll need to see them again when they come to the Artesana."

I imagine with a sudden and completely unexpected pang of jealousy that Jaume might have had something more intelligent to say—or at least a more articulate sheen of bullshit. Surely they would have come here together at some point.

Where has that come from? I'm desperate to avoid more psychodrama, particularly as we seem to be getting on again, and the easiest way to avoid it is not to provoke her. So I stick Jaume away in a dank hole at the bottom of my mind. He'll have plenty of company there.

Beatriz is still smiling, though. "I never liked them either," she says. "When you've got a city with Picasso, Miró, Dalí, why would you bother with this?"

Somewhere there's an irony that we both hate the paintings whose existence brought us together and is now keeping us apart.

"Have you got to get back?" I say. "We could have a coffee."

She does the Beatriz pause and then nods. "There's a café out the back."

And so there is, but it's packed. "Foof! Perhaps we... Just come back to the flat if you want."

I hadn't actually been angling for that, but I'm not going to say no either. We cross the road and turn the corner, and already we're on Carrer del Tigre. The Moroccans are out on the street playing their hip-hop. I know their names by now and I give them a wave. "*Hola,* Scotman," grins one of them, Ibrahim.

I trip-trap up the familiar stairs behind her. It feels like going back in time, although it's only just over a week since I've been there. She flicks on the aircon; the room's baking.

"Sit down," she says with an embarrassed shrug. I've half-lived there for months, and neither of us is clear if I'm a guest or a resident now.

I slide onto the sofa. "I thought you had to be back at work."

She shrugs again. "I told María I had cramps. They're not expecting me this afternoon."

I ponder this for a moment. "Do you have cramps?"

"No."

"*Bé.*" I grin.

"It's just...I don't know what to say to you, and I don't know how long it will take to say it. I didn't want to be worrying about the time too."

She puts a coffee pot on. I start to get up to help, but I don't want to be too proprietorial. This was never my home, and certainly not now.

We're separated by the breakfast bar as she looks over at me. "Tomàs, where do we start?"

I hunch forward on the sofa, my arms on my thighs. "I didn't mean to make you feel...I'm sorry if..."

She slides my coffee across the bar and hops up to sit on the tiled surface, looking down at me like a capricious sprite.

"I am still angry with you," she says. "Angry and hurt."

I pick up the coffee and return to the sofa. "So tell me why you're angry."

"I trusted you to... to be honest with me." She doesn't meet my eyes.

"I was. I've never lied to you about anything. Certainly not about how I feel."

She picks over this for a moment. "And did you tell me everything I should have known?"

"As much as you told me," I say carefully.

She shakes her head in frustration. "I want to know I can trust you. And I don't."

I get up and walk over to the window, glancing down into the street below. "I can't make you trust me. Either you feel it or you don't. The songs you sent me are pretty clear about where you stand."

She jumps down from the worktop and joins me at the window. "Tomàs, I am asking you now." The sun streaming through the window catches her eyes, but I still can't read them. "If I trust you, if we put this behind us, will I regret it?" She looks away. "If we mean anything to each other, can I trust you?"

I breathe out slowly, softly take her chin in my hand and turn her face towards me. "Yes. Beatriz, I will never intentionally do anything to hurt you." And for the first time I believe it, because I've had the idea that will get us out of this.

She pulls my head forward and we kiss. Somehow, this is going to work out. "You know where the bedroom is," she whispers.

PART SEVEN
13–17 AUGUST 2014
INTO DUST

1

I DON'T GO BACK TO CATFISH ALLEY THAT NIGHT, SO THE FIRST TIME I'm alone is when Beatriz goes to work the next morning, presumably to solicitous inquiries from her colleagues about her cramps.

I make myself a big pot of the now excellent coffee in the cupboard and throw together a ham and cheese croissant. I'm not out of the woods yet. I still have the interview with Rosell to come, and although he can't seriously think I had been directly involved in Ignacio's beating, I remain a person of interest to him. Since I can do nothing beyond stonewall at the interview, that problem isn't necessarily going to disappear.

My plan to get out of the whole heist imbroglio, while retaining the money, my security and Beatriz's affections, is not quite a sure thing, and still requires me to get hold of the access codes. I wonder whether now is the time to be open with her about what I'm doing, and just ask for the codes. I'm confident I can make sure the heist never happens, so I would no longer be making her an accessory to a crime. But the underlying problem remains: I'd have to confess that we only got together in the first place because I'm catfishing her, and I can't see any way of having that conversation that doesn't end our relationship. I'll have to carry on, reluctantly, manipulating her for her own good, if we're ever to come out the other side of this. And yes, I know exactly how 'manipulating her for her own good' sounds. But here we are.

I don't have my laptop with me, but I do have my own user profile on Beatriz's. I log on and open my Gmail account, creating a new document to save in the drafts, the safest place I can think of to hide it, to log what I do and don't know about how to get into the Artesana.

I know where the key to the outside lockbox is—on Beatriz's car key fob, which she hasn't taken with her today. A trip to the local *ferreteria* will solve that problem. I've also been with her a couple of times when she opened the building up ahead our film shows. I haven't got the whole code, but I know it's six digits, the first two probably being '31' and the final one '0'. There's another number pad to get into the gallery section of the building, and I have no idea of the code for that, and there's a main office which controls the CCTV.

I'm no nearer to getting the code for the second pad, or the remaining digits for the outdoor lock, but my plan won't work without them. I could give the Russians duff codes, but that's nowhere near as effective a solution. I still need Beatriz to tell me the real codes. Today is the thirteenth of August, and the exhibition opens on the twenty-fifth; I'm running out of time, and I doubt the Russians will be keen to receive the codes the day before.

There's no point in searching the flat again. She doesn't keep the codes written down, so she either knows them by heart or they're behind the passwords on her laptop or phone.

. . .

We're on the sofa that same evening, watching some awful Catalan soap opera that Beatriz seems to enjoy. I can't follow what's going on, beyond a lot of flouncing and slapping, and I reflect that most of the cast are worse than Estel. I'd given her the Ferrero Rocher—last of the great romantics—and she's eaten them all despite declaring them "repulsive". She's now moved on to tortilla chips.

"Don't look at me like that! I skipped lunch!" She's the only person I know who can eat tortilla chips without making crumbs—I am faring less well—and she looks up and says, "You know, we should get you on the committee for the social club."

I pause in my crunching. Why haven't I thought of this?

"Don't look so stunned," she says. "You'd love it."

My experience on Student Union committees suggests otherwise but that counts for nothing when I realise that committee members *have the access codes to the Artesana.*

"There's a vacancy since Gonçal left," she continues.

"Don't you have to be Catalan or something?"

"I don't see why. And Jaume is always a *fill de puta* when I'm there."

A frisson washes over me and then it's gone. "I'd be happy to help put that *poca merda* in his place." I can now confidently call someone a little shit in Catalan.

Can it really be that simple?

"The next meeting is September," she says. "I'm sure the others will want to vote you on."

September. So it's not that simple.

"That's ages away! I could start sooner."

She laughs. "Easy, tiger! You're keen all of a sudden. Is it the chance to put one over on Jaume? Montse is away for all of August, and I think Mèlia is too. You will have to control your impatience until next month."

I force a grin and reach for the tortilla chips.

The next morning is the interview with Inspector Rosell. Beatriz displays only mild curiosity on the subject but I can see it working away behind her eyes. She kisses me with unusual fervour when she leaves for work. “Text me,” she says.

I meet Hannah at Cafè Viena in good time and together we walk to the Mossos d’Esquadra building in Eixample, an unattractive square tower block. But then I suppose police stations aren’t supposed to be attractive, most of all to suspects. The last time I was here it was to report my wallet stolen. Now I’m on the other side of the law. I wonder where that pretty policewoman is now.

We’re a few minutes early so Hannah lights up a cigarette while we go over the possible course of the interview.

“It might be easiest,” she says, “if you just ‘no comment’ everything. Rosell has no evidence, and Ignacio has some shady associates. I’m also pretty certain they don’t suspect a Russian connection,” she says. “So make sure you don’t give him one.”

“How do you know they’re not already on to it?”

She stubs her cigarette out on the wall. “Rosell is just a regular detective. Organised crime is a different branch. If they thought the Russians were involved they’d have taken it away from him by now. Come on, it’s time.”

Inspector Rosell has changed his beige garments for grey today, and the windowless interview room is a couple of degrees too hot. One of the walls is clearly set up to allow observation from the room next door, but I doubt I warrant that level of interest.

Rosell seats us on schoolroom-style plastic chairs that are slightly too small for comfort and goes away to pull some coffee out of the machine, which proves to be as vile as it looks.

Once the introductions are complete he looks at Hannah. "Senyora Layton? I don't think we've met."

"I don't normally deal with criminal matters," she says with a sweet smile.

"On account of her client not being a criminal," I interject.

"And Inspector," she continues, "I must insist that the interview is conducted in English. Senyor Chisholm speaks almost no Catalan, and it is contrary to his rights to interrogate him in Spanish when it is not his first language."

I have no idea if this is true, but Rosell shifts in his seat. "Very well," he shrugs. He opens a file and looks through his notes. "Your name was familiar, Senyora, and I couldn't remember why. Here it is in my file—you, too, are an associate of Senyor Fuentes, according to Carmen Cerda."

"I am Senyor Chisholm's *advocat,*" she snaps. "If you intend to interview me as a witness, I have a conflict of interest and we will have to discontinue this conversation now. If that's what you want..."

Rosell gives a cool smile. "I am only remarking on a coincidence."

"It's not a 'coincidence'," I say. "I'm not a criminal, and I don't have a suite of bent lawyers on speed dial. So when, as an innocent man, I'm drawn into a criminal investigation, I ask the only lawyer I know to represent me. I've already said I knew Ignacio; Senyora Layton moves in the same circles."

"Thank you for clearing that up," says Rosell, sipping his coffee and grimacing.

"Have you been able to get a statement from Senyor Fuentes yet?" asks Hannah in an uninflected voice. In the humid room she's the only one who's not sweating.

"Alas, the doctors are keeping him in a coma. They've warned me there's every chance he will never be able to testify. If he regains consciousness he may not remember what happened. But Senyor Chisholm will know that since he tried to visit Senyor Fuentes in the hospital."

He was bound to have found out about that. Hannah gives me a sharp glance.

"Is that true?" She looks as if she can't believe I'd be so stupid.

"I wanted to see how he was, OK? I took him some chocolates. And I didn't find out anything anyway because Carmen chased me off."

"You didn't think," says Rosell, "that if you were a suspect, you should have stayed away?"

"Obviously not," I snap.

"Inspector," says Hannah smoothly, "if anything, this underlines my client's innocence. A criminal would not have presented himself at a guarded hospital ward. He was merely concerned for his friend's wellbeing."

Rosell grunts. "Did you know, Senyor Chisholm, that he had a lengthy criminal record?"

"I've already told you; we weren't close."

Rosell is clearly weighing that up against me visiting Ignacio in hospital.

"Six months in prison for cheque fraud, various arrests for petty crimes, a couple of assaults on women that never came to court. Suspicion of blackmail. Not a pleasant character, senyor."

"He always paid for his round, and he could chat about football. Cheap tickets for Espanyol. That's all I knew, and frankly, all I cared."

Rosell flips open another buff file. "Our notes on Senyor Fuentes suggest a possible link with organised criminals in the city."

I avoid looking at Hannah with an effort. She's wrong about them knowing that, at least.

"Do I look like a person who knows about organised crime?"

"I try not to judge on appearances, senyor."

"I don't see," says Hannah, "how this is remotely connected to my client."

Rosell scratches his hair. "Let me be frank with you both."

I prepare myself for an obvious lie.

"In my department, we don't deal with organised crime. ACCO, the organised crime unit, come in and throw their weight around, badges, guns, flashy cars. Maybe they even call in the Special Intervention Group, real hard men. An old-fashioned Barcelona cop like me, I can't say I like them too much."

"I'm still waiting for the relevance," says Hannah.

Rosell puts his palms out in a calming gesture. "My boss, he's all about clearance rates, workloads, keeping the politicians happy. He'd really like this to be an organised crime case, then we can just pass it on ACCO. Looks much better than an unsolved case on our books, which is what I have now."

"So?" Hannah's frostiness is nearly offsetting the room's heat.

"So, give me something which makes it an organised crime case. Tell me about Senyor Fuentes' other friends and associates. You, Senyor Chisholm, might even be involved, in which case I can assure you that coming clean now is much your best course."

The remark falls into the heavy air. I can sense Hannah shifting beside me.

"What's it to be, Senyor Chisholm? A few little pointers to organised criminals and you can say goodbye to me forever. My boss is happy, ACCO are happy."

"I must reiterate," says Hannah before I can respond, "that my client knows nothing about organised crime. He is a respected foreign writer, who is unfortunate enough that his friend was attacked in an unprovoked street brawl. And at a time when his girlfriend, a woman of spotless character, was with him."

Rosell nods slowly. "So it would appear. It looks like my boss will have to live with unhappiness." He leans forward.

"And do you know what, senyor? He may have believed, or wanted to believe, all this organised crime stuff, but me? No way. This feels more—domestic—to me. I mentioned Fuentes was a blackmailer. Surprising how often that gets out of hand, and it's the blackmailer who ends up in hospital."

"Fucking A," I say. Rosell frowns in perplexity.

"My client is noting how utterly speculative that remark is," says Hannah.

Rosell gives a half-smile as he prepares his cliché. "Do you have any enemies, senyor?"

"I'm a writer, an English language teacher, an all-round nice guy. No, I don't have enemies."

Rosell looks at me reflectively for a moment. "Carmen Cerda was not complimentary about you. She described an angry scene between her cousin and you."

"At which she wasn't present," I say. "I think that's called hearsay."

"It seems we still have several lines of inquiry," he says. "You, Senyor Chisholm, undoubtedly know more than you are saying. I can't prove that—"

"Inspector—" Hannah chips in.

"—yet. But the reason I have worked my way up from traffic policeman to Inspector is persistence. I do not give up, Senyor Chisholm. I do not give up."

. . .

With the customary injunctions not to leave town, now supplemented with a prohibition on visiting the hospital, and a warning on the seriousness with which Spanish courts viewed perjury, Rosell closes the interview.

As soon as we get outside, Hannah lights a cigarette.

"That's a dangerous man," she says. "You were right to bring me."

"He was pretty close on the—"

"Fuck, Chisholm, you want to talk about this outside the police station?"

I point to the Plaça d'Espanya twenty feet away. "That's the busiest roundabout in Barcelona. I can barely hear you, and I'm standing next to you."

She shrugs and blows out a plume of smoke. "Rosell will never give this up to ACCO," she says. "There's too much departmental rivalry, and he'd much rather pin this on someone else than give them a lead they can work with. The trick is to make sure it's not you."

"He doesn't really think it is."

"That doesn't mean he won't tie you to it if he thinks he can. You're lucky you've got a reasonable alibi. If it came to court, Beatriz Bernat would be a convincing witness. Carmen Cerda is not so fortunate."

"Do you know her? No-one can seriously believe she had Ignacio beaten up."

Hannah shakes her head. "I didn't have the kind of relationship with Ignacio where he introduced me to his family."

"See, I dumped her, and I admit I was a shit to her—"

"No..."

"—but she's actually a nice girl. I wouldn't like to see her framed for something we both know she didn't do."

"You can't look after all the waifs and strays in the world, Chisholm. It's a bit late in the day to develop fucking chivalry.

You want to keep Carmen out of trouble, you want to keep this Beatriz tramp out of trouble. Wake up, sunshine! The Russians did this to Ignacio, and if you get out of this with your hide and your money, you've done well. Sometimes you have climb over the bodies to get where you want to go."

I say nothing.

"Don't look at me like that, Chisholm. The twenty-fifth is not far off and you need to deliver. Now fuck off home and get on doing what you've been paid to do."

2

I SEND BEATRIZ A TEXT TO SAY THAT THE INTERVIEW WITH ROSELL went ok, there's no more evidence, and that I hope that's the end of it. I'm more worried that she'll kick off about it when she gets home than I am about what Rosell might do now.

For once I get a lucky break. Beatriz is brimming with excitement once she gets back to the flat. Galeria Petritxol has had a late cancellation and they've offered her the space for Saturday and Sunday. She's in no mood to probe too deeply into Rosell's investigation.

"There's so much to get ready! Will you help me choose the pictures? It's only the small gallery so I can only have about a dozen."

I don't think the Petritxol has done her any favours: a poky room, no time for proper publicity, and it's the middle of August when Barcelona is all but empty. There's no way I can say that without looking like I'm sneering or belittling what she's achieved, so I just help her pick the best pictures out of the loft studio at the top of her building. If anyone comes through the doors, I'm sure the pictures will sell.

. . .

I've misjudged how pragmatic she is about the whole thing.

"I'm doing them a favour," she says as we stand on her balcony looking out over the street with glasses of rioja. "They don't want an empty space, and we've agreed that if this one goes well they'll let me have a bigger exhibition next year. If I sell anything this time, it's a bonus."

It's not the first time I've underestimated her. I ought to learn to stop doing it.

We spend all Friday evening setting up the gallery ahead of the opening on Saturday. The Petritxol itself is an understatedly attractive building in a classy Eixample location, actually not that far from the Artesana. It's on a narrow pedestrian street, fronted with sober buff stone, and although the room set aside for the exhibition isn't large, it has an airy feel and the lighting is magnificent. It's a serious space, and I can't help feeling a little emotional as we work out the best way to arrange the pictures, and how many we can fit in without it feeling crowded.

I can't help but notice that the security measures are negligible. If anyone wanted to empty the Galeria Petritxol, a crowbar and twenty minutes would probably be enough. A shame they would never be given a Llussà Moncada exhibition.

Estel looks in during Saturday evening, subtly nudging potential buyers and pointing out interesting features in the work. All the rest of our group are busy this evening, but they've arranged to come in the next day and go for drinks afterwards.

. . .

By Sunday evening, when the exhibition is winding down, we're able to evaluate it as a success. Three pictures sold on the first day, and another two today—nearly a thousand euros in total, and definitely enough to warrant another show next year. There are still a few potential buyers in the salon when Estel and the rest turn up.

"I can't believe you've put all this together so quickly," says Aleix.

"I couldn't have done it without Tomàs," says Beatriz. "I may have to employ him as my assistant."

I bask in the compliment. Really anyone could have helped hang the frames on the hooks and give an uneducated opinion about what looked best where. But that's not the point, and we all know it.

"It's astonishing," drawls Jaume, all in black, "how much difference professional lighting makes. Even the most mediocre work would dazzle in these surroundings!"

Salut, who it seems is no longer talking to him, gives him a look of utter disgust. I feel an urge to punch him which I control relatively easily; Beatriz puts a hand on my arm. She's clearly not upset by him, and after the weekend we've had, why should she be? The exhibition has been a success by any standards, and I'm delighted to see her glowing with confidence. For now, at least, I can set aside my worries about her, and even the Russians.

The gallery director turns up at closing time. Estel and Aleix have already gone on ahead to Broadway, and Beatriz says I might as well wait outside while she settles up, so I'm outside on the pavement with Jaume, who's pacing up and down, impatient for Salut's emergence.

We eye each other warily. I'm really no threat to him—the only woman I'm interested in he's already dumped—but he can tolerate no rivals on his territory. And for any number of reasons, I'd quite happily push him under a bus.

He sniffs. "She was lucky to get this exhibition, don't you think?"

"She made her own luck," I say. "She spent long enough lobbying for it, and if her work hadn't been good enough, they wouldn't have taken her."

Jaume shrugs. He's recently given up smoking, and he carefully unwraps a stick of nicotine gum and puts it in his mouth. "No-one wants an exhibition in August. It's dead time for the gallery. They'd have taken anything at short notice."

"They couldn't have taken anything of yours, then. Estel told me the one thing you ever produced was shut down by public health."

He pauses in his chewing. "True artists have always been in conflict with authority and doomed to be misunderstood." He flicked his head towards the gallery. "These days they prefer illustrations to real art."

"From what I was told, your installation was a collage of used condoms and tampons?"

"I wouldn't expect you to understand. It was a meditation on the reproductive cycle."

"You weren't censored. That's not what the public health department does."

Jaume flicks some fluff from his jacket sleeve. "Barbarians and philistines."

"Why are you so jealous of Beatriz's success?"

He grins. "You call that success? A couple of hundred euros

for something she could have copied off the internet? You have to say that you're screwing her."

I take a step towards him. "You are getting on my fucking tits, pal."

He draws himself up, a couple of inches taller than me. "Oh yeah? You know she's only with you because I didn't want her? She's nothing special, as an artist or a woman."

I take another step towards him. His eyes are ablaze with a mocking light.

"You're welcome to her," he says. "You're the perfect couple – a graphic designer with pretensions and a failed writer."

"And yet you still hang around with us all, almost as if no one else will tolerate you."

Behind us, Beatriz and Salut are coming out of the gallery, with farewell kisses on the cheek for the director. Jaume leans forward and whispers in my ear.

"Don't pretend you're any different to me. I can see through you. These girls, they're all sluts. I help myself and so do you."

Beatriz puts a hand on my arm. "Sorry we were so long. Is everything OK?"

I compose my expression. "Fine. Jaume and I were just discussing love and life."

Her face freezes. "I can't think you'd have much to say to each other on that."

Jaume laughs. "You'd be surprised."

"You stay out of my relationship!" she hisses.

Jaume spits his gum on the pavement and raises his hands in mock alarm. "Hey, we were just having a man to man chat. Men talk, you know." He leers at the pair of us.

Salut has been watching with a face of silent disgust. "Jaume, will you stop it! Just leave them alone!"

He makes an exaggerated bow. "For you, anything."

"Fuck this," I say. I reach out for Beatriz's portfolio. "Here, let me take that. Estel will have got the drinks in by now."

I lead the way down the road towards Broadway, taking Beatriz's hand.

"What was that about?" she asks.

"You don't want to know. He's a little shit, but I don't think that's news to you."

She sighs. "No. But at least I appreciate it now I have something better." She stops in the street and kisses me. Back up the street, Jaume and Salut appear to have got into an argument.

"Should we go back?" I say.

Beatriz shakes her head. "Salut can look after herself. We usually can, you know."

I grin. "I never doubted it. Come on then, or Estel and Aleix will have drunk Broadway dry."

3

Aleix and Estel have got a couple of bottles of cava sitting in an ice bucket. The upper floor of Broadway is humming without being too busy. It feels like our own private reception.

Beatriz is glowing. I try and find a tingle of envy, because she is now more successful than I am, but I can't. I see how hard she's worked for this, and how much she deserves it. The two pieces she's sold today, one for two hundred euros and the other for five hundred, are in a large portfolio case by her side so that she can get them framed for the buyers.

One hand is resting on mine, and for the first time in weeks I'm starting to feel relaxed. It's all illusory, because the Llussà exhibition starts at the Artesana next week and I'm no closer to the codes, but tonight I feel that everything is going to work out.

Estel's play has come to an end, but she has an audition for a part in a soap opera.

"You're sure to get it!" cries Beatriz when Estel tells us.

"Well, I don't know," says Estel. "A two-year contract would be nice, but there will be lots of people after the part."

"You're better than any of them," says Aleix. "No-one realises how talented you are."

Estel looks at the bottom of her glass, which is now empty. Beatriz drapes an arm around my shoulders. "Go and get us some more drinks, Tomàs. We are all thirsty."

I indicate the bottles of cava, which are not yet exhausted, with my head.

"Let's have cocktails," says Aleix. "We must celebrate Beatriz's exhibition and Estel's audition."

I catch Beatriz's eye. "Anything but a mojito for me. A Manhattan maybe," she says.

I ease my way up to the bar—it's getting more crowded now. A man with a glass of beer jolts into me and liquid slops down the side. He scowls.

"Sorry. *Perdona.*" I say reflexively. It's as much his fault as mine, but the evening isn't going to be improved by a bar fight, and he's both taller and more muscular than me.

The guy shrugs. He's got dark curly hair cropped close, five o'clock shadow and tattoos on his neck and his decisive hands.

He smiles and makes a dismissive gesture. "Hey, don't worry," he says in heavily accented English.

He's not going to be an arse about it, so I say, "Here, let me get you another," since I'm already at the bar.

"No need," he says, holding the glass up to show only a little bit missing off the top.

"Two Manhattans, an Old Fashioned and a daiquiri, *si us plau.*" I say to the barman. "And another beer for my friend."

"Thank you," he says with a nod. He looks over to where the others are sitting. I may have bought him a beer but I'm not going to invite him to sit with us.

"Your friends?" he says.

I nod, just this side of curt.

Beatriz is looking around, wondering where I've got to. She catches my eye and smiles.

"And your girlfriend?"

"Yes." *So don't be getting any ideas, pal.*

"She is very beautiful."

I can't deny that, and neither do I want to.

He grins. "You are a lucky man, my friend."

This isn't a subject I want to get into with a stranger.

"Where I come from," he says, "the girls, they do not look like this."

"I'm sure they're beautiful in their own way," I say. "There must be pretty girls everywhere."

He shrugs. "Perhaps, but in Spain...wonderful!"

It's true the Spanish girls, with their vivacity, their golden skin and musical voices, impress me more than the ones I grew up with in Kilmarnock, but this guy has never been anywhere near Ayrshire.

"So where are you from, that the girls are so ugly?"

He grins and takes his beer off the tray the barman has just put on the counter.

"Russia." He takes a sip from the glass. "Thanks for the drink. Have a good evening, cowboy."

And with that he's slipped into the press of bodies.

I can literally feel cold sweat in my armpits. He knows who I am. He knows who Beatriz is. He hasn't had to utter a word of a threat. There's no need.

I take the tray over to our table on numb legs.

"Tomàs? Are you all right?" says Beatriz. "You look worried."

"I'm fine."

"You do look pale," says Aleix.

"I'm Scottish, what do you expect?"

Beatriz puts a hand on mine. "Tell us." I've no chance of

convincing her everything's OK. She's far too perceptive and she knows me too well.

"The guy at the bar was a dick," I say. "He bumped into me and then kicked off. I had to buy him another drink to shut him up."

"Ah," says Estel. "Don't worry about it. He'll think he's the big dog and that's all he wanted."

"I know," I huff. "But I didn't want Aleix to have to rescue me."

Aleix laughs. "He wouldn't have known what hit him. Although it's Estel he should have been worried about!"

"I don't know what you're implying," says Estel, taking her daiquiri from the tray.

I lift my Old Fashioned. "To Beatriz. And Estel. The two most talented women in Barcelona!"

We clink glasses. The moment of tension has passed, but only for now. For the first time I seriously consider going to the police. Surely Rosell isn't bent? He might even welcome the chance to drop a solved case in the ACCO's lap. If I can't get the codes by tomorrow, I'm going to have to think about it, now they've made it clear they know about Beatriz.

"You're miles away, Tomàs," laughs Beatriz. She kisses me. "You can't be bored with me already."

I feel a catch in my throat. There's nothing I won't do to protect her.

"Look, I have an idea," I say. "It's crazy but we have to do it!"

"Crazy ideas are always the best," says Estel, "especially when we're celebrating."

I point to Beatriz's portfolio. "Let's go to the Artesana," I say. "They don't move the Llussàs in until next week. We can hang Beatriz's paintings there and take pictures of them. The Petritxol is a nice gallery but they will look so much better hung in the Galeria!"

Beatriz slaps my arm. "That's a ridiculous idea."

"Why not? We can post the pictures on your Instagram later," I say.

Estel laughs. "Why not? What else have we got planned for the evening?"

"You've got the keys and codes, right?"

Aleix frowns. "Well, yes. I've got my key. But there's other security, surely."

"CCTV, infrared, but you can switch all of those off from the main office."

"You are well informed," says Aleix with a thin-lipped smile.

I shrug. "I watched *The Thomas Crown Affair*," I say. "I can't imagine the Galeria has better security than that."

Beatriz shakes her head, but it's in amusement at my idea rather than opposition.

So an hour later we're at the door of the Galeria, Estel fishing in her handbag for the key to the number pad. The building is completely dark, and the streetlamps clump a yellowish pool of light around us.

"Hurry up!" says Beatriz, levering her own keys out of her jeans pocket. She unlocks the case.

Estel, who is a little drunk, leans against the wall next to the keypad. Beatriz sighs and types in the code, but her hand is obscuring the pad and I still can't see the numbers.

"You might as well tell me the codes," I say casually. "I'll be on the committee in a couple of weeks anyway."

"I can't remember them to tell you," wails Estel. "How am I going to learn my lines for the audition!"

"You probably saw that one anyway," says Beatriz. "The inside ones..." she pulls out her phone.

"Ahem!" says Aleix. "They are security codes for a reason. We don't just tell our friends when we feel like it."

"Aleix!" says Estel. "This is Tomàs! Of course he should have the codes."

"And next month he will," says Aleix primly. "Once he is voted on to the committee."

I watch the pair of them. If Estel wins I'm home free.

"So Jaume has the codes but I don't," I say. Chucking that wee shite's name in must help. Everyone here hates him.

Aleix frowns. "That's not the point. It's still wrong, and we all know it."

"When did you become such a teacher's pet?" says Estel. "I'll tell him and you can pretend not to listen. The gallery space is two...er...two...one? Oh, I can't remember."

"Both of you be quiet," says Beatriz as we step inside the darkened foyer. "We can get in now, Tomàs doesn't need the codes tonight and he's not going to be coming here by himself anyway. Let's just wait for the committee meeting."

I try not to let my disappointment show. The codes I only want so that I can help Beatriz are now out of my reach because of her own comments. But her take is unarguable. There's no point in my having the codes tonight, here with three people who already know them (two if you discount puggled Estel) and so the whole debate is void.

"Come on," Beatriz says, lighting the way with her phone. She punches one code into the main office—possibly six digits but I can't see any of them.

Beatriz disengages the internal alarms using another code I can't follow, and then we push through the main doors into the gallery space. Estel turns on the lights—the room has no external windows—and I take in the bare white walls. Whatever had hung here previously has been taken down in preparation for the arrival of the Llussàs.

The rest of the night is a total waste of time for me. I'm only here for the codes, and despite my best efforts, I still don't have them. But Beatriz is so excited when we hang her prints on the gallery wall, posing for photos in front of them, that I can't really regret it. Two prints are not enough for the gallery space, but we can crop the photos later.

She kisses me on the lips in front of the two prints while Estel takes a picture on her phone. "Thank you! This was such a lovely idea. I feel like a real artist."

I smile back wanly. I'm all heart. "You are a real artist, B," I say, my voice catching. "You must always believe that."

She draws back and looks into my face, sensing some deeper emotion than the situation calls for. She strokes my hair. "I love you," she whispers. I pull her close to me; there's nothing I can say.

PART EIGHT
18–19 AUGUST 2014

DON'T KISS ME GOODBYE

I

THE NEXT MORNING, I SEND HANNAH A TEXT ON HER BURNER PHONE, IN direct contravention of her earlier instructions.

We need to fucking meet ASAP

It's half-past six—Beatriz is still asleep—and I don't expect a response. It's an hour later, when Beatriz is in the shower, that my phone vibrates.

Are you out of your fucking mind?

Progress update. Its important

9-30, Viena

And so when Beatriz asks me as she's leaving for work what my plans for the day are, I'm not lying when I say: "Meeting with my lawyer, in case there's any update from the police."

She nods. "Good luck. See you tonight."

Cafè Viena is only a quarter-hour's walk from Beatriz's flat and I'm there well ahead of time. Although it's only just gone nine, Barcelona heat in August is punishing, and it's already sticky. I'm a bit hungover from the previous night, and Barcelona in high summer is not the best place for a sore head. The light which has inspired artists for centuries will seep through even closed eyelids, and the unrelenting heat will bake your headache until it explodes. The only positive about the month in the city, other than how much easier it is to conduct an art heist, is that there are far fewer tourists. Even many of the locals make themselves scarce.

Hannah, who has presumably fought her way down here on the metro, is nonetheless cool and unruffled as she saunters through the door. She sets her handbag down on the seat next to her and orders an iced coffee.

"So," she says. "What's your idea of important that's worth me rescheduling a whole morning's appointments?"

I've already had an espresso while I waited but I signal for another.

"I'll tell you what's so important." Her own poise and assurance are just making me more agitated. "Last night I was in a bar with my friends when someone who claimed to be Russian arranged to bump into me. No overt threats, no unfriendliness, but he scared the living shite out of me. And he made a point of knowing who Beatriz was, by the way."

She sips appreciatively at her coffee. "You'd really benefit from a cold drink in this weather, and an espresso is not what you need just now. Let me order you a decaf iced."

I lean forward. "My problems are a bit more serious than fucking over-caffeination. I'm going to end up like Ignacio, or Beatriz is. You have to get them to back off."

Hannah sighs and puts her glass down. "I work for them, not the other way round. You know what they want, and the exhibition opens in a week. You can understand them getting a little—impatient."

"I have a copy of the external lockbox key, although I don't know the whole code to the lockbox itself. I can't get into the gallery space, but I understand how to turn off the alarms and the CCTV from inside the building."

Hannah sniffs. "It's not much for something you've been working on since February, but I suppose it's progress."

"I'm not going to lie to you, Hannah. I'm scared. You got me into this, you fucking get me out. People getting beaten into a coma, this was never the deal."

She says nothing for a moment and looks reflectively into my face. "For what it's worth, I'm sorry it's turned out like this. I didn't expect what happened to Ignacio, and I didn't realise how unsuited to the work you'd be. I certainly never imagined you'd be more worried about protecting your girlfriend than the money."

"Aye, well, you live and learn. She didn't ask for any of this."

"You're really in love with her?" Her expression is a mixture of cynicism and, for a second, wistfulness.

I don't reply.

Hannah shakes her head ruefully. "I gave you credit for more sense, but I suppose that's on me. But if you care about her, for fuck's sake get those codes. If the Russians think you can't come through with it, they'll snatch her off the street and get it their own way."

"I don't understand why they didn't do that to start with."

"You're not cut out for crime, are you? As soon as she reported the crime, or if she was in no condition to, the Artesana would change the codes. But if they do it the night before the heist, there's no time. I'm sure they'd prefer not to get their hands dirty, but sometimes needs must."

"Do you know," I say, "until Ignacio was beaten up, I never believed there were any Russians at all? I thought it was just you, or you and Ignacio, pulling a scam. I couldn't see why a bunch of gangsters wanted to steal paintings they could never sell on. And I never had any doubts that I could deal with the pair of you."

"The Russians are all too real, Chisholm. And you can be sure they have a buyer lined up, or they wouldn't have come this far."

I can't understand why anyone would want to buy art they could never openly display, but that's not the Russians' problem, or mine.

"Listen," I lower my voice. "Do you want out of this too?"

She leans back in her seat and inspects me. "And if I did?"

For a second I ponder telling her my plan – to get the codes, pass them on, and then tip off Rosell so that they're caught in the act. But if she doesn't go along with it, the plan's blown, and when all's said and done, I don't owe her anything. She's the one who got me into this, and surely she's on to make a lot more than thirty thousand euros. And she's a lot more distanced from the front-line than I am. She's got nothing to lose by letting it play out.

I shrug. “I don’t know. Maybe we could come up with something together.”

She touches my hand. “Tommy,” she says softly. “It’s too late for that now. Get the last codes out of the girl—or you won’t like the way the Russians do it.”

I’ve never seen her like this before. I might have found her easier to work with if I had.

“It’s none of my business,” she says, draining the last of her coffee, “but what’s she got, this Beatriz? Why is she so worth fucking everything up for?”

“I couldn’t put it into words, Hannah. And if I could you wouldn’t understand them.”

I can see the shutters come down over her eyes. Whatever rapport we might have been building is snapped.

She stands and throws a five-euro note down on the table. “And luckily not my fucking problem, sunshine. You dug the hole; you climb out of it.”

I can’t face going back to Beatriz’s flat, seeing all her things, all the evidence of our happy domesticity that we’ve built on my lies and her trust. Instead I stay in the pleasant, air-conditioned hum of the café. It’s too early for beer—I have to retain some standards—so with a wry smile I order the iced decaf coffee Hannah had recommended. It’s every bit as disgusting as I’d imagined.

I shred my paper napkin as my mind skates over my remaining options. It’s too late to run now, whether it’s Kilmarnock or the mountains. All that would do would be to leave Beatriz to the Russians and I’ve just enough backbone left to know that I can’t live with myself if I do that and something happens to her.

There’s still the option of throwing the whole thing over to

Rosell or going straight to ACCO if I can work out how to get hold of them. I'm probably guilty of some sort of crime—Hannah is the expert on the Spanish legal code and I'm hardly going to ask her—but if it shuts the whole thing down won't it protect Beatriz? I'm not sure it would work, though. I don't know who the Russians are and the only person I have any direct evidence on is Hannah, although even here I doubt our text messages are conclusive. All it would do is tip the Russians off and something tells me they aren't the kind of people who'll laugh off being clyped to the police.

My current plan, then, is still the best despite the buffeting of the past twenty-four hours. The only way for the Russians to be properly stopped is for them to be caught in the middle of the heist. Trapped inside the building with ten Mossos cars waiting outside. It's risky but I still can't see a better option.

But it only works if the robbers are inside the building. Standing out the front trying to work out the keycode is suspicious but a lawyer would get them off before it even got to court. They have to be inside the Artesana, and that means they need the code to the outer door. The code which Beatriz has and I, still, don't.

I have no napkins left to shred, so I think, fuck it, and order a whisky, which comes on a silver tray with its own individual serviette. This is no time to get wrecked, but a stiffener surely won't go amiss.

I've run out of road. There's no way I'm going to con the code out of Beatriz, or any of the others. The only option left—and fuck, I wish there was another—is to come clean. To say, "look, I've got into something over my head and the only way out of it is the code." I can't imagine how that conversation will go. I don't know whether Beatriz will explode or implode, but either way, everything between us will be over. Can I try confessing to Aleix? Or Estel? They'd both probably give up the code if they thought it would keep Beatriz safe. But they wouldn't keep it secret, and nor should they. Their loyalty is to Beatriz, not me. The least I can do, the last little shred of self-respect, is to have this conversation with Beatriz myself. And to do it sober. I push the whisky glass away and call for the bill.

2

Beatriz is late home from work, tired and snappish. I can tell just from hearing her walk up the stairs. I can put this off until tomorrow, can't I, when she's maybe in a better mood? But I know I can't. We're running out of time, and I'm not going to get any peace until we've done this.

She kisses me as she comes through the door. Sweaty and sticky from the walk from the metro station, she still smells wonderful. I'm going to miss this, so much that I can hardly bear to do it. I think of Ignacio, still in a coma. That could be Beatriz next time. I've got no choice.

She feels something awry in the way I embrace her.

"Tomàs? Is something the matter?"

My mouth is dry. I can barely speak. I shake my head. "Sit down. There's something I need to tell you." And now there's no way back.

Her bag falls to the floor from slack hands and she wordlessly moves to the sofa. There's already pain in her eyes and I haven't said anything yet. I lean against the breakfast bar, desperate for some distance ahead of what's coming.

"You're dumping me?" she whispers. Somehow I feel even worse that this is the first thing she thinks of.

"No. But you're going to be dumping me." I pause to gather my thoughts, although I've spent the last four hours thinking what I'm going to say. And once I start, I can't stop. Running out of money, Hannah, Llussà, the codes, the Russians, the consequences of failure.

She doesn't interrupt. She sits immobile on the sofa, her eyes on my face the whole time, her fingers playing with a loose thread on her jeans.

Eventually I finish. Don't believe anyone who tells you confession's good for the soul.

"That's it? That's everything?" Her mouth is a thin sharp line, her face held expressionless with God knows what effort. Her mouth is bracketed by fine lines.

I nod. I realise I'm crying and she's not. I can't even do this properly. "I'm sorry, Triz. You will never know how sorry I am."

"*Bé*. You're right because I don't want to know. I don't care how you feel."

"This would have been so much easier if I hadn't cared about you." I'd sworn that I wouldn't try to justify myself, and I couldn't make that stick either. "I've been trying to get out of this for so long, to make sure you didn't get hurt and you wouldn't hate me."

For the first time her face flicks into scorn. "And how did that work out, Tommy? Now, when you've no choice, now you tell me that you fucked me and told me you loved me so that I'd whisper the codes to you? What part of that is going to stop me hating you?"

Her voice has barely risen above a scything whisper.

"I've been trying to find a way out since the beginning."

"You know, Estel and Aleix both told me to be careful, that I hardly knew you. And I didn't find it easy to trust you, but I did in the end. I thought you *understood* me. I thought you *saw* me."

Her eyes are starting to brim now but she doesn't take them off me.

"So I told Estel and Aleix that they were wrong, that I knew what you were really like. And *I* was wrong again, wasn't I? Stupid, stupid Beatriz! I never learn and maybe I can never learn." A tear falls from one eye and she brushes it away. "I am twenty-eight years old and I still can't tell a man from a *tros de merda.* A piece of shit."

I look away and then back into her eyes. "This isn't your fault, Beatriz. This is nothing you did. I deceived you, on purpose, and I played on your good nature."

Her eyes flash briefly. "You think I don't know that? From the start!"

She draws back into herself, her mind running over all those times together, times she'd thought of as precious and special, and all unravelling in front of her.

"You have to leave now Tommy. I can't have you here, I can't see you in front of me. Come back tomorrow to get your things."

"The codes—the Russians—you are still in danger, Beatriz."

She rises from the sofa and now the dam has broken. Her voice climbs to a shriek. "You think I care about your fucking codes? You think any of that matters? Your schemes, and still you can't give them up. We're done, Tommy, finished."

She reaches into her handbag and pulls out a cylinder. "Unless you want me to mace you."

I hold up a hand. "I'm going. Asking me to leave is enough."

I edge past her, close enough to see her hand shaking. I reach out for the door handle. "This won't mean anything now," I say. "It won't make you feel any better at all. But maybe in the future it will help. I lied to you about why we were together, but I never lied to you about how I felt. All of that was true."

Her hand drops to her side. All the energy has gone out of her. "I know," she whispers. "And that doesn't make it better. It makes it so much worse."

There's nothing else I can say. I open the door and pull it gently shut behind me, on Beatriz and on the life we might have had together.

3

I CAN'T FACE GOING HOME, SO I SLINK ROUND THE CORNER TO EL GAT for a drink. The bar is a favourite haunt with Beatriz, and we've had some great nights there, so perhaps it's not the best choice, but it's there or Periquito, two minutes away, where I used to hang out with Ignacio. That doesn't feel like much of an option either and at least El Gat doesn't have those fucking budgies.

"*Hola, Xabi!*"

"Tomàs! No Beatriz tonight?"

"No, she's staying in." And that's true enough.

I order a beer and some tapas and try not to think about what just happened. Not only have I utterly torched what Beatriz and I had—that was unavoidable—but I haven't even made her safer from the Russians. All in all, perhaps the worst evening of my life.

And it's not finished yet. A figure slides into the seat next to me. "Senyor Chisholm, may I join you?"

I glance up. "It seems you already have, Inspector."

Rosell smiles, incongruous against the backdrop of eighties dance music. One of Beatriz's prints hangs sadly on the wall behind his head.

"I wouldn't have thought this was your scene," I say.

"You'd be surprised where duty takes a policeman."

"Duty? At nine-thirty on a Monday night?"

He reaches out for an olive from the tapas. "May I? In a sense I'm never off duty. Criminals don't work office hours."

"I wouldn't know."

I could really do without being needled by the sleekit wee bawbag.

"I wanted to catch you after the weekend," he says, dipping his olive into some aioli. "I was just about to come to Senyoreta Bernat's flat when I saw you come out. Perhaps better this way."

"Is this a formal interview, Inspector? Do I need my *advocat*?"

"We can make it formal if you like, go back to the station, drag Senyora Layton away from whatever she's doing. Or we can just have a chat in a bar, two lonely guys on a quiet Monday night."

"I'm not lonely," I snap. "I have a girlfriend."

Rosell looks around the small space theatrically. "I don't see her here now."

"She has a headache."

"Ah, don't they always?"

"I doubt you've come here to give me relationship advice, Inspector."

"I thought you would be interested," Rosell says, wiping his moustache with a napkin, "to hear that Senyor Fuentes has woken up."

"Pleased, certainly. You had implied he never would."

"Modern medicine is truly remarkable. And the resilience of the human body."

"I didn't have you down as a philosopher."

"Would you like to know what your friend said when he

woke up?"

I push an empty plate away. "You're dying to tell me."

"In fact, no," says Rosell with a half-smile. "Maybe when we have that formal interview, with Senyora Layton there to ensure the British fair play, maybe then we can discuss that. You might want to think about admitting what you've done before you're trapped by his statement. Looks better in court, you know."

He nods in evident satisfaction as he bites down on another olive.

"So that's not what you want to talk to me about?"

"Not just now." He smiles again.

"Xabi!" I call. "Another beer please, *si us plau,* and whatever the Inspector's having."

Xabi's eyebrow rises at the thought of me fraternising with a cop.

"Beer for me too," says Rosell.

He turns back to me. "I don't sleep too well," he says. "My mind races, I can't switch it off. As a writer, maybe the same for you?"

"Not so much," I say. Although plenty of other things keep me awake.

"Always cases with me," says Rosell. "Little things whirring away in the back of my mind, tick tick tick. No wonder I can't get to sleep."

I've come to realise that circumlocution is all part of Rosell's technique. There's no point in trying to hurry him.

"I'm thinking about your alibi, Senyor Chisholm."

"It's not that complicated. I thought we'd established that I was with my girlfriend, which you either believe or you don't." I hope to Christ he doesn't want to talk to Beatriz again. With what she knows now I'm screwed if she comes out with it.

Rosell shrugs. "Because Senyoreta Bernat is your girlfriend, she'd say anything to keep you out of trouble."

"You clearly don't know her very well, Inspector, and I thought I was a witness, not a suspect." This is wishful thinking and we both know it.

Rosell leans forward and whispers confidentially: "Everyone's a suspect, Senyor. Everyone."

"I'm thinking maybe we should call Hannah Layton."

"Hey, five more minutes. I checked your criminal record. Clean, in this country at least."

"Equally clean in Scotland, let me tell you."

"Then I checked Senyoreta Bernat's."

I can't hold back a laugh. "You're not telling me she's got a record?"

"A couple of speeding tickets, no more. But guess what else?"

"It's been a long few weeks, Inspector. Just tell me."

"It's probably nothing. She's on our list of keyholders for the Galeria Artesana, in Eixample. You know it?"

"Sure. She's on the committee there, I've been with her a couple of times, taken in some exhibitions, watched a play."

"Do you follow their programme of events?"

"Not closely."

He reaches into his jacket and pulls out a flyer. Sliding it across the table, he said: "What do you make of this?"

I know what it will be, and I'm right. In fact, Beatriz designed it. It's the programme for August, headlined *Special Exhibition: 'The Forgotten Surrealist: Llorenç Llussà Moncada'*.

I push it back. "Apparently next week," I say. "Beatriz mentioned it. She's not a particular fan and neither am I."

Rosell takes a sip of his beer. "Forgotten for a reason, eh? But it prompted a theory in my mind when I couldn't sleep at three a.m. You're a writer. Think of it as an idea for a novel."

I'm horribly fascinated by this. Rosell is perceptive and my guts are roiling at the flyer on the table between us. It's all guesswork, but he's frighteningly close to the truth.

"I've got a Scottish writer, no money and no visible means of support. His girlfriend, an artist of sorts, although she doesn't make any money either. Job just above the minimum wage. And a petty criminal who knows plenty of other petty criminals. Who just happens to have a conviction for blackmail. Another one for handling stolen goods."

"I'm listening," I say carefully. The only previous conviction Rosell had mentioned is for cheque fraud. Blackmail had only been a 'suspicion' last time. He's been trying to lure me into this from the start.

"The two who think they are clever, they see that MACBA is lending the Artesana the Llussàs for an exhibition. The girl has a key to get in, she knows the art world, she maybe even knows who collects them on the side. And the man, he knows a criminal, someone who can help them move the paintings on."

"So far, so speculative. And so preposterous."

"The three of them hatch a little scheme. But it's a mistake to trust the crook. He knows you'll never get away with it, and for him blackmail is much easier. So he turns the tables. It's the two of you who are now in trouble. Do you know how people generally deal with blackmailers, Senyor Chisholm?"

"Never having been blackmailed, no I don't, pal," I snap. I pick up my glass but it's empty.

"One of two things. Either they pay, and you and the senyoreta are broke, so you can't do that. Or they try and scare the blackmailer off. They never do the third thing, the sensible thing, which is go to the police. So you only had one choice, Senyor Chisholm. You beat him up, or you have him beaten up, and unluckily for you he nearly dies. And even more unluckily, he wakes up. Head injuries, so hard to get right."

"I was with Beatriz, Inspector." I've never previously understood the term gritted teeth can be literal.

"We've established you can't prove that Senyor Chisholm. And if she's your accomplice—well, you might as well have no alibi at all."

"This is bullshit, Rosell. It's all speculation, all circumstantial evidence, and it's not true. Whatever Ignacio has said, it won't have been to do with this."

"You don't sound very confident."

"I am completely confident. I've done nothing, Beatriz has done nothing."

Rosell shrugs and pops the last olive in his mouth from the remaining plate. "Like I say, think of it as the plot for a novel. You can use it if you want."

"You're all right, pal."

He stands up and wipes his lips again with his napkin. "You're right about one thing, Senyor Chisholm. I can't prove any of this – not yet, at any rate. But understand this—one way or another, I always get a conviction. One way or another... well, you'd better have Senyora Layton on speed dial. *Bona nit, senyor.*"

As he leaves I signal Xabi for another beer. Suddenly my mouth is dry.

It's frightening how close Rosell has come to the truth. All the details are wrong—and Ignacio can't have implicated me because he doesn't know anything, so that's a bluff—but the Llussàs and the exhibition at the Artesana, Beatriz's access codes... this is an extra complication I didn't need. Rosell will not only have his eye on me—and on Beatriz—but also on the Artesana. But the Russians are still pressing for the codes, and if I warn Hannah that the police are on to us, they are only going to blame me. The best solution is still to let the robbery go ahead and tip off the police at that point. Once the Russians are caught, it's ACCO's case, not Rosell's. They won't be interested in his non-evidential theories about me or Beatriz, even if Rosell is minded to help them. I still, just about, have the opportunity to play the police rivalries off against each other.

It's all academic, though, because I still don't have all the codes, and now I have no way of getting them. There's no prospect of Beatriz helping me. Should I, could I, just trust Rosell after all and tell him the whole thing? Everything comes down to trust. Beatriz had made the choice to trust me, and how had that turned out? And what are Rosell's motivations? Justice for Ignacio? A tick-box on his clearance rate? Getting one over on ACCO? And more than once Hannah implied that the Russians have eyes in the local police. If that's true, I'm just putting my neck and Beatriz's in the noose.

The Germans have a word for it, of course. They always do. *Zugzwang*, a position in chess where every move open to you makes the situation worse. The optimistic Spanish have no equivalent term in their own language, but I'm in a Barcelona Zugzwang, right enough.

So what's the least worst option? Do nothing—always a good starting point. It keeps me out of Rosell's clutches, but the Russians will hurt me, or worse, Beatriz. Confess the truth to Rosell—too many unpredictables, a certain criminal conviction for me, and no guaranteed safety from the Russians. Come clean to Hannah—not even worth consideration, she'll fuck me over in a heartbeat. Tell Beatriz about tonight's conversation and beg her for the codes—she can't despise me any more than she already does, and it stands the best chance of keeping her safe if the Russians are caught in the act.

I'd been intending to slip into her flat when she was at work to collect my stuff. But now I'm going to have to talk to her. *Frightened of talking to a girl, Tommy? More frightened than how you'll feel if the Russians kill her?*

I slide my phone out of my pocket to text her, praying she hasn't blocked me.

Need to pick up my clothes. Can we talk tomorrow?

A pause, dots. It's almost like speaking to her in real life.

Come when I'm at work, leave the key when you're done

I need to talk to you

There's nothing to say

I promise I won't try and talk you into getting back together. I know it's over

Then what's to say

Please B, much easier in person

Trust me, I add, and then delete it before I press send. That's the one thing she'll never do.

There aren't even dots at the other end now. I don't blame her. In the circumstances I wouldn't be meeting me either. Just when I've given up there's a beep.

8-30. Then you stay out my life forever

OK

I don't even get round to typing the kiss before I scrub the idea.

Although this is exactly the response I need, I also want to shake her for being so stupid. Letting a man she's just dumped, with a history of lying to her, come into her flat on his promise of good behaviour? I've never shown the slightest inclination to violence, but it's still not sound judgement. I can't switch off the part of me that wants to take care of her, but it's almost comically inappropriate here. All I can do now is live up to the implied belief in my self-control.

• • •

I finish my beer, say goodnight to Xabi and walk out into the street.

4

As it turns out, Beatriz has been more sensible about her security than I imagined. I walk down from Baixada del Silur, the heat already beginning to bite at eight a.m. and traffic fumes squatting in the heavy air, to find myself ten minutes early.

I doubt that she'll be asleep, so I unlock the outer door and walk up the stairs. I knock on her flat door—even though I've still got the key I can hardly barge in like I still live there.

Seconds later the door is open and my head is ringing from the biggest slap I've ever received: Estel. She follows it up with a string of low rapid muttered Catalan that I've no chance of following, although the message is clear enough.

She stands aside from the door and makes a sarcastic bow to let me in. Beatriz is on the sofa in the same clothes she was wearing last night. Neither of them looks like they've been to bed. On the armchair are two black bin bags, which I assume are my clothes.

Estel is by the window looking at me with undisguised loathing; Beatriz isn't looking at me at all. I don't know where to stand, Estel being in my favoured position, and I can't sit next to Beatriz, so I stand drooping next to the door.

Beatriz looks up, dragging her attention back from wherever it had been before.

"So. You wanted to talk. I need to be at work, so make it quick."

"Beatriz—" My ingenuity falters.

"I told you," says Estel. "There's nothing he wants other than to hope you'll forgive him. Begging like a whipped dog."

"This is nothing to do with you," I say.

Estel barks a dismissive laugh. "It isn't? You lied to all of us, all year. You might have hurt Beatriz the most, but you owe all of us an apology."

A harsh smile flicks out before I can stop it. "I think we're past apologies, although if it helps, yes, of course I'm sorry. I didn't have to say anything."

"Oh, so we're supposed to be grateful that at the last minute your conscience decided letting the Russians hurt Beatriz wasn't worth thirty thousand euros to you? *Fill de puta!*"

So she's told Estel everything. I can't really blame her, although I'd rather she hadn't.

"Estel." Beatriz's voice has the weariness of centuries. "Let him speak, then he's gone."

"Inspector Rosell cornered me after I left here last night," I say, taking a deep breath. "He knows some of the truth, he's guessed part of what he's missing, and is plain wrong about the rest. But he's suspicious."

Beatriz shrugs. "*Bé.* He's a policeman. What do you expect?"

"I don't know how to make this any more persuasive, but the only way to keep us safe—to keep *you* safe—is for me to pass on the codes so that the Russians can be caught when they hit the Artesana."

They are both silent. "And I know you wouldn't be in danger

if it wasn't for me in the first place, but I can't change that now."

Estel shakes her head. "What a man. What a man."

Beatriz reaches into her handbag and pulls her phone out, pecks at her passcode with shiny nails clacking on the screen and taps a couple of icons.

"You want the codes so badly. Here are the fucking codes."

I realise a second too late what she's doing. "No, Beatriz, don't send them to me—write them down!" But it's too late. She's pressed the button, and instantly my phone beeps, the codes glaring out from her screenshot.

"There, are you happy? Was that worth putting up with having to fuck me all summer?" If her mouth wasn't so dry I think she would have spat at me.

I sag down onto the armchair on top of my pathetic clothes bags. "You shouldn't have done that," I say. "If the Artesana is robbed, Rosell will pull my phone records, and probably yours too. And now they show you sending me the codes."

"*Merda.* Shit, he's right." This is Estel.

"So I don't give him the codes, I'm a stupid bitch? I do give him the codes and I'm still a stupid bitch?"

"Beatriz—"

"B—"

"What, you're ganging up on me now? Estel, you're supposed to be my friend!"

She walks over to the sofa and hugs Beatriz. "Ssshhh. *He's* the problem, and we'll deal with him together."

By now I'm completely out of ideas about how this can be dealt with at all. Beatriz texting me the codes has destroyed the only way I could have kept her out of it.

"Beatriz," I say. "I'm going to go now. I've only made things worse. But if you only believe one thing, believe this: nothing about how I felt this summer was a lie. It might not have had a happy ending—" Estel lets out a howl of incredulous laughter "—but it was all real."

Beatriz looks up from where she's slumped against Estel. No-one's interested in how I feel, and I can't blame them.

"*Bé*. Goodbye."

The thought of my flat is intolerable, so I slump outside a nondescript café and call for a coffee. There's no positive I can put on this: I'm absolutely fucked. It's not as if I deserve any better, but worst of all, I've now dragged Beatriz into it as well. Ironically, I've solved the original problem—key and codes all ready to hand over to the Russians—but if the robbery goes ahead Beatriz is unbreakably tethered to it by phone records. What possible way out of this is there?

My mind goes back to last night's conversation with Rosell. *They never do the third thing, the sensible thing, which is go to the police*. I can't fix this myself, and while Rosell might be disappointed to hear an explanation involving organised crime, which cuts him out of the picture, it has to be better than any of the alternatives. Doesn't it? Or does his determination to keep organised crime away suggest he has a vested interest in protecting the criminals?

I look down at my phone and see a missed text from Hannah from while I was at Beatriz's.

Viena. Now.

Her manners aren't improving, but Hannah isn't someone I'd ever expected to show grace under pressure.

5

If I think the unpleasant surprises for the day are over, I'm wrong. Hannah is sitting inside the Viena when I arrive, and next to her is a face I recognise: the Russian goon from Broadway.

Her eyes flick up as I approach the table.

"This is Ilya," she says in a cool emotionless voice.

Ilya looks up at me with a half-smile which scares the shit out of me. Even Hannah looks pale, and I've never seen her even slightly rattled.

"Sit, my friend," says Ilya. "I am sorry we didn't talk more on Sunday. Today, we talk properly."

The waitress brings over coffees for Hannah and Ilya, and I order one of my own. Ilya leans back in his seat and downs his espresso in a single movement.

"Now," he says. "The time for fucking around is over, cowboy. Key, and codes."

I try to catch Hannah's eye, but she's studying the surface of her coffee as if something is floating on it.

"I hope," says Ilya, his voice conversational and uninflected, "that you don't think you have a choice. You have been paid, my friend. Now it's time."

I'm not your fucking friend, pal.

"I told Hannah I didn't have the codes." I can feel the sweat seeping through my shirt. I could just hand them over, but that's a one-way street. For now, at least, I have the power of knowing something they don't.

Ilya leans forward. "The wrong answer." He cracks his knuckles. "I thought Senyora Layton had told you what would happen if you made us unhappy."

I reach into my jacket and pull out my copy of Beatriz's outer door key and slide it across the table.

"That will get you inside the building."

Ilya pockets it in a movement almost impossibly swift and deft for such large hands. "Not enough, cowboy. Codes as well."

"I said, I don't have them."

Ilya picks up his espresso cup and, with a single decisive movement, slams it down on the table, cracking the china. "I don't like liars."

"No, well—"

"Chisholm," says Hannah.

"I told you already," I spit at her.

"I didn't believe you either."

Ilya toys with the pieces of china on the table in front of him. "You would rather not annoy me," he says mildly. "Your address, 27 Baixada del Silur, no?"

I lick my lips. "That's not a secret."

"Beatriz Bernat, 24 Carrer del Tigre."

"Leave Beatriz out of this."

Ilya smiles to reveal crooked white teeth. "I would like to, my friend. But that depends on you, of course."

I look up to the ceiling for inspiration, see only a drowsy wasp circling. I don't doubt Ilya is willing to hurt Beatriz if he has to. Maybe even if he doesn't. I'm mad to think I can play power games with people this ruthless. I'm a fucking amateur by comparison.

I pull my phone out and open my texts to reveal the codes Beatriz sent me. "Copy them down," I say. "I'm not texting you."

"Pen," says Ilya to Hannah, who scrabbles one out of her handbag. Ilya quickly jots the details on the back of the bill.

"Not so hard," he says. "Next time, you don't lie, hey?"

Hannah looks across at me. "You shit-sucking fucker," she says. "You had them all along."

"She's only just given them to me," I say.

"Whatever."

I stand up. "So are we done? I never have to see the pair of you again?"

Hannah treats herself to a grin. "What about the rest of your fee, sunshine?"

I'm tempted to tell her to stick it, but this whole thing has so comprehensively fucked my life up that I might as well least get all the thirty pieces of silver I've earned.

"You know how to get hold of me."

And there is of course the fact that Rosell being so close to the truth means that the robbery is not going off without a hitch anyway. But this isn't the time or the company to mention it.

PART NINE
19—22 AUGUST 2014
DARKHORSE

I

I SET OFF TO WALK BACK TO CATFISH ALLEY. IT'S ALREADY GETTING uncomfortably hot, but I can't face the press of bodies on the metro, and I always think better on foot. And I have plenty of thinking to do.

The Russians now have everything they need to allow them to carry out the heist. In that sense my job is done. But for all I know Rosell has a watch on the Artesana, and even if he doesn't, the first place he will come after the robbery will be Catfish Alley. And then he'll pull my phone records, and Beatriz's, and we'll be on the hook for the whole thing.

"Watch where you're going," snaps a woman with a pushchair as I dawdle along the street. I hold up a hand in apology.

I really don't trust Rosell, and I still can't be sure that he's not on the Russians' payroll. Despite that, he might yet be the least worst option, if I can find a way to keep Beatriz out of it. If I've learned nothing else, it's that I'm not cut out to be a criminal. A fucking shame I didn't realise that in February.

. . .

My phone is understandably quiet over the next couple of days. I'm finished with Hannah, and the people I care about in Barcelona—not just Beatriz, I realise, but Estel, Aleix and the rest of the group—now all hate me, and I can't blame them.

I'm still asleep at nine a.m. when I hear the phone beep, and blearily I reach out. Estel! Surely there's nothing she has left to say to me.

You have a new problem. Meet me after work tonite.

Whats this about, Estel? You aren't interested in my problems.

This one affects all of us. Meet me at 7.

She sends me directions to a bar in Barceloneta, near the railway station, not one we've been to before. I still don't know what she wants, but there's only one way to find out. I doubt it's to my advantage.

She's already there when I arrive, nursing a Coke. From the neon sign on the front to the sterile furnishings inside, the place is a soulless horror. I find myself pining for the earthier charm of Periquito.

"You choose the nicest places," I say, ordering a beer.

She shrugs. In her work clothes, her hair clipped back in a barrette, she looks like someone I don't know.

"We're not on a date," she says through lips that barely

move. "It's next door to work, and I prefer to meet you in a public place."

I settle down on a stool next to her at the bar. "So how are you? How's Beatriz?"

She eyes me like a cockroach that has got into her apartment. "Really, Tommy? After everything?"

"Whatever I've done," I say, toying with a beer mat, "it doesn't mean I don't care. You have to believe me; this was all a terrible mistake."

She pokes at the ice in her drink. "'Mistake'? The famous English understatement."

I let the nationality pass. Even I can see now isn't the time to be an arse.

"You don't want to be friends. I understand that. So why am I here?"

She sighs. "The Artesana has introduced a new security measure ahead of the Llussà exhibition. They texted us all last night. The codes won't be enough to get you into the gallery."

Just what we need.

"And you're telling me because?"

Her cheeks colour. "Because whether we like it or not, you've put all of us in danger. We need to hold our nose and work together."

"I'm not holding my nose."

"No. But I am. So is Beatriz."

"Just tell me about the new security, give me the codes to that, and we're back on."

Estel purses her lips. "Not so simple. It's biometric security, a fingerprint scanner. We all had to register today."

I feel a wave of dread. "So—one of you needs to be there with the Russians?"

She nods.

"Can't you get me on the list? I could go with the Russians."

"Only committee members."

Shit. For a moment the wild idea of cutting off Jaume's finger amuses me.

"You think this is funny?" she hisses.

"Sorry," I say. "In no way is this funny. Look, can't we just go to the police?"

She leans back on her stool. "That puts you in trouble," she says. "And obviously, I don't care. But Beatriz texted you the codes, so she's involved too. I do care about that."

I stare listlessly into my beer. "What are we going to do?"

"I'd come with you myself," she says. "I still would, but Beatriz—"

"What about Beatriz?"

"She thinks it's her fault. Her mistake in trusting you. So she's going to do it."

"*Merda*, Estel! Beatriz isn't a gangster! These are dangerous people."

"You haven't left her a lot of choice," she sneers. "You've put her in danger, Tommy. You can hide and writhe and squeal all you like, but you have put Beatriz in a noose. Now you have to do something about it."

"Like what?"

"Make it right with the Russians. Beatriz goes along, and you go too."

I shake my head. "This is impossible."

"If you don't do it like this, you think they won't snatch one of us? Probably Beatriz anyway. This way, you still have some control, some power."

I run a hand through my hair. I seriously think I might vomit over the bar. "This is really better than going to the police?"

"Aleix, Salut, Mèlia—we will all give Beatriz an alibi. I will make sure of it. We will say she texted you the access codes because you were going to be on the committee. Stupid, but not criminal."

"And me? My alibi?"

She pauses for a second. "You deserve to go down with the Russians."

"That's my price. I'm not sending myself to jail just to make you happy. Any alibi you give Beatriz, you give me too."

"*Price?*" she spits. "You want to be rewarded for this? You are putting Beatriz's life in danger and you want us to protect you?"

"Estel—"

"You are a snake! You'll get your alibi, and I hope it makes you happy."

I miserably rip my beer mat in half.

"And Tommy—if this goes wrong, you don't need to worry about what the Russians will do. I'll kill you myself."

2

Estel told me to phone Beatriz after work. She doesn't want to meet me apparently, and while I understand that I don't see how the heist will work without us being in the same place at some point.

It also occurs to me, as I sit on the roof terrace above my flat working up the nerve to call her, that I've never spoken to her on the phone before. We've been intimate in every imaginable way, but phones are just for work. Your friends, you text. But I suppose we aren't friends any more.

I call up her contact details, to which I'd assigned a photo of her sitting on the beach at Sitges in a bikini and sunglasses, looking impossibly cool. Christ, was that only June?

I take a sip of the whisky I've brought up to the terrace with me—from a glass, I have standards—and push the green icon to call her. It rings twice and she doesn't pick up, so I make to hang up. She obviously doesn't want to speak to me after all. But then the ringing stops: a moment of silence and then—

"Tommy?"

Her voice is flat, tinny. Her accent is much stronger over the phone.

"Yes. It's me. Beatriz, how—"

"Estel told you about the new scanners?"

"Yes."

"Talk to your gang. I'll go with them."

"They're not—"

"This isn't a conversation. Tell them that, find out where I need to be and when. That's all you have to do."

It's not just the phone speakers which are deadening her voice. There's a lack of inflection, a brutal suppression of empathy.

"Beatriz, can't we talk? This could be dangerous for you."

She pauses, but over the phone it's not the same. I can't see her mind working.

"You should have thought of that before you got me into this."

"You think I don't know that B?"

The phone signal is not great—Jesus, I'm on top of a building, Movistar is the world's worst mobile provider—but I think she's crying.

"Listen," I say. "When it happens, I'm coming too. I can't let you do this by yourself."

Silence.

"Beatriz?"

"Whatever. I don't care. If it makes you feel better. A man."

"I'd rather they were pissed off with me than you."

I can feel the shrug over the line. *Bé.*

"Call me when you know the details," she says and hangs up.

I stare at the phone as her image dims and it falls silent. It had been like talking to a stranger. Nothing I can ever do will make this right. It's the only time I've ever made a proper connection with someone, and I've burned it down to the ground. Well done, Chisholm.

I realise with a grim lurch of the stomach that I'll need to brief Hannah, and perhaps the brutal Ilya, on the new security. I can't imagine either of them will be delighted at such a major change of plan so late in the day.

3

I'm right about that if nothing else. It's Thursday evening, and we're in Broadway, Hannah, Ilya and me. The venue feels like a deliberate insult, the place where I'd hung out with my friends and been happy, in another life, last week.

"You can trust her, this Beatriz?" says Ilya, his black eyes drilling into me.

"She hates me—"

"—surprising—" interjects Hannah.

"—but she'll do it. She knows it's in her best interests. She only needs to touch her finger to the screen."

"I still don't see why you need to be there. This is not a game."

I lean back and take a sip of my beer. "She will be less scared if I'm there. You don't want her to panic."

Hannah smirks. "And you're the best friend she has? Poor girl."

"I'd have thought," I say to Ilya, ignoring Hannah, "that you'd want me there. A guarantee of no police, at least."

Ilya leans forward. "Senyora Layton has told me you are not

intelligent. But even you, Senyor Chisholm, are not so stupid that you don't know what we'd do to you."

I shoot Hannah a glance. Her gaze is level. "If you were as bright as all that, Chisholm, you wouldn't be in this mess."

Ilya drains his beer. "I'm not doing this with a stranger," he says. "Call her, get her here."

"What, now?"

He leers. "You don't want the big night to be our first date, hey, cowboy?"

"For Christ's sake! She might be busy, she might..."

Ilya shifts uncomfortably in his seat. Not a man used to being contradicted.

Hannah puts a hand on my arm. "Call her, Tommy." Her eyes flick across to Ilya. "Seriously, this isn't worth an argument."

I nod, take my phone out, and stand up.

"Where are you going?" asks Ilya.

"I'm calling her from outside. I don't need you two looking at me, and it's too noisy in here."

Ilya looks like he's going to say something.

"Do you want her here or not?" I snap. "Let me do this my way."

Ilya cracks his tattooed knuckles and shrugs. "As long as she's here in half an hour."

It's still light outside, with a warm breeze that does nothing to take the temperature out of the moist air.

"Beatriz?"

"You have the details?"

"Kind of. Can you come to Broadway?"

"Now?"

"Yes. One of the Russians wants to meet you."

There's an agonising pause.

"Do I have a choice?"

Now I pause. "No. I'm sorry, Triz, but you really don't have a choice at all."

"Fuck you," she breathes down the line.

"Look, I know it's not ideal—"

"Fuck you! *Fill de puta!*" This time she screams it.

"These people are professionals. We do our jobs, everyone's happy, we go home."

"Tommy." Her voice drops. "I'm scared."

I bite my lip. "I know, Beatriz. I'm scared too. Whatever I can do to get us through this—both of us—I will do it."

It's hardly reassuring because we both know my influence over the Russians is zero. We're well past me getting brownie points for good intentions.

"Just come down now, OK?" I say. "You know Broadway, it's busy. Nothing's going to happen."

"I'm on my way." She hangs up without saying goodbye. Maybe she doesn't know how to.

I can tell as soon as she walks in that she's terrified. I'm the best friend she has here and that's a good enough reason. Ilya leers as she approaches the table. Hannah gives her an appraising once-over.

I make a space on the banquette next to me. "This is Beatriz," I say unnecessarily. "These are H—"

"No names," says Ilya.

Beatriz swallows and sits gingerly next to me. She looks awful. Her eyes are puffy, her skin pallid under the tan. She has a rough patch at the corner of her mouth where she's gnawed her lip. She's lost inside a large grey hoodie.

"So," says Hannah with a smirk. "You're the famous Beatriz.

How lovely you could join us. I've wanted to meet you for so long."

Beatriz gives me a sideways glance. The thought of me reporting back to Hannah about her is clearly an unwelcome one. I see her start to fold in on herself, then she leans forward.

"Well, I've heard plenty about you, *senyora*, and I can tell you I've never wanted to meet you," she hisses.

"Oh, you have a feisty one here, Chisholm," Hannah purrs. "Maybe she'll do after all."

"Enough," says Ilya. "All of you, get your phones out, turn them off."

"You think we're recording this?" I say. "We'd only incriminate ourselves."

"Phones. Off." Ilya is not a man to tolerate dissent.

We all get out our phones and put them on the table. Beatriz fumbles hers and it drops at my feet. I reach down to pick it up as she dives for it, and for a moment our heads touch. I get there first and hand it to her.

"Thank you," she mutters.

Our phones off, Ilya starts to speak.

"OK, now the details. Senyoreta Beatriz, you know why you're here? What we're doing?"

The leering flirtatiousness has gone from his manner. It's all business now.

Beatriz nods.

"We go first thing Monday morning," he says. "We meet here, airport car park, long-stay, floor six, 02:30."

A map goes down on the table, a location circled. "Beatriz, you know where that is?"

She picks up the map, studies it. "Yes."

"We get in the van, we drive to the target, park round the corner. Beatriz, you have a key to the outer keypad and the codes?"

"Yes."

She's settled now, following Ilya's businesslike tone.

"You open the front door, we all go in. Where is the new fingerprint sensor?"

"The door to the main gallery."

Ilya nods. "I am standing next to you. You use the sensor and the keypad. The guy who's with us goes to the main office, turns off the CCTV and the picture alarm system. There's no other security to this point, right?"

"No."

"Good. The three of us go into the gallery, take the pictures off the wall, put them into the holdall. We walk back out the way we came, load the van, drive off, and we're done."

"Hang on," I say. I can see Hannah watching us through narrowed eyes. "Where am I where all this is going on?"

"At home playing with your dick, what do I care?" says Ilya.

Hannah sips her drink with a half-smile.

"No," I say. "That wasn't the deal. I'm there. It was agreed."

I look at Hannah who gives a "what can you do" shrug.

"No, no," says Ilya. "This is serious business. No passengers, no amateurs."

"Beatriz is an amateur."

Ilya gives a sharp smile. "But not a passenger. She has a job."

"This isn't right," I say. "You can't expect Beatriz to do this by herself." My palms are sweating.

Ilya looks me up and down. "You're going to protect her, hey?" The contempt washes off him.

"He comes or I don't," says Beatriz in a surprisingly firm voice.

Ilya leans forward. His leer is back. "You think you have a choice, girl?"

She pushes her chin forward. "You need me."

Ilya shakes his head and grins. "I need your finger. The rest of you is optional."

Hannah chuckles. I've never hated her more.

"Do you want him wandering the streets while this is going on?" says Beatriz. She gives me a brisk distant glance. "He is a weak man, with half a conscience. Do you want to take the risk that he won't call the police? He'll do whatever seems easiest at the time."

"She's not wrong, is she?" laughs Hannah. "God, what did you ever see in him?"

Ilya ponders for a moment. He inspects Beatriz. "OK. You've never done this before, maybe it helps keep you calm. And Chisholm, yes, let's keep him where we can see him."

Is that really what Beatriz thinks of me? Hannah leans forward and taps her on the arm. "You were wasted on him, dear."

Beatriz leans back and hisses "Don't touch me! I know what you are."

Hannah laughs. "Oh, Chisholm, what a little Spanish spitfire! And so far out of your league."

"And what will you be doing, while all this is going on?" I say with the closest I can come to a snarl.

"Me? Sunday evening? Oh, probably a long hot relaxing bath with a mud facial, while you busy beavers are off making us some money. I want to look my best for work on Monday."

"You will need more than a mud facial, then," says Beatriz. "The sun is cruel to northern skin, particularly on older women."

I cough. Ilya is openly laughing. "This one, she'll do," he says.

Hannah stands up. "Are we done here? All clear on our jobs?"

"Yes," says Beatriz. "An early night—good for the complexion. You are very wise, senyora."

I've never seen this Beatriz before, and despite the circumstances I like it.

"It's late," I say. "Can I walk you home?"

She looks at me with the pause of all pauses. Something has changed inside her. She's found a confidence from the desperation of the moment.

"OK."

4

Beatriz and I walk down Carrer de Muntaner, the broad pavements allowing us to be level but not touching. Both the fear and the hostility seem to have gone out of her. The streetlamps catch her hair.

"Beatriz," I say, looking down at the ground. "I know you must hate me—"

"I don't hate you," she says in a flat voice, also not looking at me. "You did what you did, I trusted you, I was wrong. That's all. You disappointed me."

I stop walking and she has to do the same. "I never meant for any of this to happen."

Now she looks at me. "But it could never have been any different. What did you think, all these criminals would go away and leave us to be happy?"

It sounds ludicrously naïve when she says it like that. "Yes," I say. "I was stupid, but that's what I thought."

I put a hand on her arm. "I wanted it so much, you know, I thought that would make it happen."

She shakes my hand off and starts walking. "Estel said I

should have gone to the police as soon as you'd told me what you'd done."

I run a hand through my hair. "She's probably right, by the way."

"I was worried about the Russians, what they'd do to me, to Estel."

"And to me?"

"No, Tommy, not to you. What's the English, you make your bed, you lie in it?"

I can't blame her for any of this. "I never thought you'd be in danger. The fingerprint sensors, you know, you should have never had to be there. If I'd known it would turn out like this, I swear to you, I'd have..."

She shakes her head ruefully. Her eyes are moist. "It doesn't matter, does it? On Monday morning, they're robbing the Artesana, and we're doing it with them."

We're outside her flat, and she gets her keys out of her purse.

"Why did you let them take me as well? You didn't have to."

She turns the key in the lock. "I needed to show them I wouldn't be pushed around, that they needed me more than I need them."

I nod. She flicks the quick half-smile I've missed so much. "And also, if it goes wrong on the night, they'll kill you before they kill me."

"Christ, Beatriz, no-one's getting killed."

She opens the front grille and the door behind it.

"Are you coming in or not?"

I can't think of a coherent response.

"I have work tomorrow," she says. "I'm not standing out here all night."

I troop up the stairs behind her. Whatever has happened

tonight, it's completely retooled the dynamics of our relationship. All the confidence, all the control, is hers. I'm just the sap who does what he's told. She seems to be enjoying it.

It's only two days since I was last in her flat, but it was another world. Any sign I ever lived there is gone, and there's a smell of disinfectant. She's literally cleaned every trace of me out.

I shut the door behind me. She turns to face me, slaps me hard.

"I should have done that on Monday," she spits. "You dog! *Fill de puta!*"

I rub my cheek. I can hardly complain—I've earned that, and plenty worse. She leans towards me and kisses me just as hard on the lips.

"And *mare de Déu*, I've wanted to do that too."

I return the kiss and we're scrabbling at each other's clothes.

"Beatriz—"

She puts a finger on my lips. "*Shhhh.*"

Afterwards, in the bedroom I thought I'd never see again, she's looking into my face.

"What just happened there?" I say.

She sits up and pulls her knees into her chest. "I used to think you were an incredible man—kind, handsome, intelligent. You know, I thought you were too good for me."

I run a finger across the back of her hand. "And now?" I know I'm not going to like this bit.

She shakes her head. "Now I see the other side. Weak, cowardly, manipulative. And that's OK. It's just how you're made, and I don't have to worry that you're too good for me anymore."

I can't argue with any of this.

"And us?" I say.

She laughs. "There is no 'us', Tommy. What just happened, it's the end, not the beginning. On Monday, we do the job, I hope no-one gets hurt, and then it's over. All of it."

I sigh and stroke her hair. "I'm supposed to get paid at the end of this," I say. "Thirty thousand euros. Half the money, if you want it—it's the least I—"

She jerks away. "You think I want money? That I'm a fucking *puta*, a whore? *Merda*, Tommy, that's not what this is about!"

I put my hands up to ward her off. "I didn't mean that. It's just—I feel like you've earned it, you know?"

She shrugs. "Maybe I have. But I don't want it. If you think the Russians will ever pay you, good luck. But even if they do, I don't want the money. I'm not a criminal, even if you are."

I stand up from the bed and reach for my shirt. "I'm sorry, Beatriz," I say. "Do you want me to go?"

She looks at the clock—it's two-thirty—and pauses to reflect, gently shakes her head. "No. It's too late now. Stay. Stay."

I'm awake before Beatriz—in fact I never went to sleep—and as it soon as it's light I slip through to the kitchen and make some coffee. I notice with a pang the red and yellow Café Bustelo tin which I'd bought and left there. Happier times...

After some hesitation I make pour two cups—just a dash of milk in hers, two proper Scottish sugars in mine—and take them through to the bedroom.

"Sorry. Did I wake you?"

She peers at me through the half-light, then flicks on the bedside lamp. "You're really here?"

"You did invite me."

She ponders that for a second. Tentatively I take her hand and she doesn't pull away.

Sitting up, she takes her coffee. "What are you going to do today?"

"You're really interested?"

She shakes her head. "I have work today. If you've got nothing planned, go to El Corte Inglés, get us some black hoodies and scarves to cover our faces."

"For?"

She looks at me as if I'm half-witted.

"For Monday. Unless you want to wander round the Artesana with your face out until we turn the CCTV off."

I'm both impressed and horrified at how easily she's slipped into the practicalities of managing an art heist. I've never known her at all, have I?

"You know what size I am?" she asks.

I've never really understood Spanish clothing sizes.

"Forty?"

She sniffs. "Their clothes come up big on me. Thirty-eight will do."

I nod. "OK. I'll drop them off before you get home."

She squeezes my hand. "You can stay here. Until Sunday. I don't want to be alone before."

I look into her eyes, try to work out what, if anything, is behind the invitation. But her expression is a blank. I'm starting to think the only thing worse than not being reconciled with Beatriz is being reconciled with her.

. . .

Mid-morning finds me in the cafeteria at El Corte Inglés. I've never liked shopping or department stores, but El Corte, with its views over the city from the cafe window, is a different experience to the soulless hell of East Kilbride or Livingston. And you wouldn't get *churros* like these in Scotland, I think, dipping the pastry into the sweet chocolate gloop that accompanies them.

On the seat next to me are two white carrier bags with their green and black triangles: a pocket flashlight, two hoodies, two scarves, plus some black jeans for me. If I'm going to do this, at least I'll be colour-coordinated. On impulse I picked up a bangle fashioned into an elongated cat shape for Beatriz, although I don't understand why. I also have a cheap Alcatel pay-as-you-go phone. Beatriz doesn't know about that, and she doesn't need to. I've got more fucking phones than a drug dealer.

I take out my iPhone, look up Rosell's number and transfer it into the contacts of the new phone. Everyone except me has forgotten about him—Ilya has probably never heard of him, while Beatriz and Hannah have only met him once each. But I'm front and centre of his suspicions, and it wouldn't surprise me at all if he's following me. It will be beyond a bollock-ache if he turns up at the Artesana on Monday morning.

There's only one way I can think of to avert it, other than coming clean about the whole thing. And if there's ever been a moment for that, it's long past.

The cafeteria is filling up and a middle-aged woman with brassy blonde hair and even more bags than me sits down at my table without a word, looking at my two phones with disfavour. I glare at her. *You don't like my peaches, don't shake my fucking tree.*

I slip the iPhone back into my pocket and carefully compose a text in Spanish on the Alcatel.

You were right about the Artesana. It's being robbed 02:30, Tuesday

This is a risk, but the phone's going into the sea after and the SIM card down the drain in pieces. Whatever Rosell might suspect, he won't be able to trace the message back to me. And he'll be ecstatic at the thought of turning up on Tuesday to catch us all red-handed, either with or without ACCO.

Whatever police business Rosell is engaged in this morning, he drops it immediately.

Who is this?

It doesn't matter. The information is good.

Senyor Chisholm?

Forget who I am

Come in and talk to me. It will be better for you in the end

Tuesday. 02:30. Don't be late.

. . .

I flip the back off the phone, take the SIM card out and snap it in two. I drop the pieces in the sludgy residue of the *churros.* The woman opposite me stares in detestation.

I pick up my bags and slide out of the cafe.

5

"We can't sit in here until Sunday," I say after Beatriz comes home.

"No," she says, sitting on her sofa in the black hoodie which is a perfect fit. The new bangle, which she'd accepted without a word, is on her wrist. "Let's have one last weekend, before we—"

"—go to jail—"

"Before we say goodbye."

I can't read her expression.

"An art heist. That's some goodbye," I say.

"You know there can't be anything afterwards."

"I know. The police, they'll be trying to make connections."

The look in her eyes is almost pity. "Nothing to do with the police. You and me—Monday, it's over."

I'm starting to wonder whether that's true. I can't deny I'm not boyfriend of the year material, but it's not been completely my fault, and is she beginning to see that too? The experience has changed her—she's harder, more brittle, maybe more worldly now—but she doesn't seem to hate me. Some part of her, maybe more than that. But we can park the future until after Monday. If that goes wrong, the future is a box with bars.

"I'm hungry," she says. "Let's get something to eat at El Gat."

We steer clear of the mojitos, but it's almost like old times. If I look closely, I can see a hint of wariness, a lack of spontaneity, so maybe the answer is not to look too closely in the first place.

Xabi is working tonight and he comes over with some drinks. "Haven't seen you two in here for a while."

I shrug. "Busy with work, you know."

"I thought maybe..."

Beatriz reaches over and puts her hand on mine. "No, nothing like that."

Xabi grins. "Good." He slips back behind the bar.

It's starting to fill up, and we're having to shout to be heard over the music and the crowd.

"Come outside," I say. "I want to talk to you."

She pops a couple of banknotes under her empty glass and we press through the crowd to get outside. I catch a glimpse of a familiar face: Rosell. He meets my eye and nods. I take Beatriz's hand and slip past without acknowledging him.

"You look like you've seen a ghost," she says as we step out into the cooler evening air.

I shake my head. "It's nothing."

She gives me the look of a person who now distrusts everything I say.

"So what is it?"

I put my arms around her waist, draw her towards me and inhale the scent of her hair. "Not now," she says.

I step back so that I can look into her eyes. Even with the lamps outside the bar, they are unfathomably dark.

"On Monday, your job is to open the Artesana with the fingerprint sensor, right?"

She sticks her hands in her jeans pockets. "You know it is."

"Presumably, that's linked up to some kind of computer system, a server that's somewhere else."

She looks down at the ground. "I wondered when that would occur to you."

"So when the police come to investigate, they'll be able to tell that your fingerprint was used to get in."

She looks back up. "Yes. I should think so."

"Rosell already suspects you. You're in big trouble, B."

"Yes." Her face is blank as marble.

"I've put you here."

"Let's not do this again. You said you're sorry, just forget it."

"How can we? We need a plan."

She turns away, and a ruffle of breeze catches her hair. "If you'd trusted me with this at the beginning..." The cry bursts out of her. She rubs both hands across her cheeks and turns back to face me.

"You want to know the plan?" she says. "This is the plan. I will have an alibi from Estel, Aleix, Mèlia. And you, for what's that worth. If I need it, Xabi will say I was here on Sunday night. There's no CCTV, they can't check. And then my lawyer claims the fingerprint sensor was hacked. And I am clean, neat, polite. I've never been in trouble with the law. The judge will believe me."

I lean back against the wall, a drainpipe digging into my back. "And do all these people know they're providing an alibi?"

She shrugs. "Estel does. The others will do it because they're my friends."

"Friends who'll be committing perjury."

She takes a step towards me. "That's on you, Tommy! It's because of your fucking lies, your—"

I hold up two hands. "I know, B, I know."

She moves back and her mouth curls into a grin. "And if that doesn't work? If my lawyer says it's not practical, or someone says no to giving me an alibi? Then I tell the truth: that you coerced me into it. And I won't have any regrets about it, none at all."

Her head is one on side, her expression truculent and challenging.

"Jesus, B, I don't blame you. If you have to do it, do it. I'm in deep enough water anyway. If it gets that far, there's no point in me denying it, right enough."

Her eyes narrow. "I hope I can believe you, otherwise I've given my defence away."

I take both of her hands. "I know you don't trust me. And I know why. But now, no more secrets. There don't need to be."

She looks at me for a long moment. "I never had any secrets. They were all yours."

7

We spend Saturday and Sunday doing touristy things together. The weather is perfect, and we stroll up and down the Ramblas, visit the cathedral, walk round the Park de Montjuïc where Hannah had paid me the first of the money. I don't think I let go of her hand the whole day. Perhaps I can't bear the thought of her leaving me behind.

Finally we make our way to Broadway for an early dinner. As ever, we go upstairs and watch the world unfolding on the floor below us. We've been here so often it seems unimaginable that in a couple of hours we'll be in the middle of an art heist. I have a Corte Inglés carrier bag containing our hoodies and black jeans, ready to get changed when the time comes.

I try to gauge Beatriz's mood. She's quieter than usual, studious and composed. I don't sense any sign of panic or wanting to back out. The single-mindedness she brings to everything, from her art to relationships, is pitched on tonight, and doing what she needs to do to get out from the hole I've dug for her.

The food is good at Broadway but we've both hardly touched our plates. Our drinks—Coke for me, mineral water for Beatriz—are equally unloved. Beatriz doesn't wear a watch, so she's constantly looking at her phone to check the time, which seems to be running backwards.

"Come on. Let's go and get changed."

We slip into the toilets, re-emerge in our matching black outfits. "Twins," I say. She looks at me wonderingly and shakes her head.

"Showtime," she says softly.

PART TEN
24—25 AUGUST 2014
ONLY LOVE CAN BREAK YOUR HEART

I

I CAN FEEL BEATRIZ TREMBLING NEXT TO ME AS WE TAKE THE LIFT UP TO the sixth floor of the airport car park. I flip my hood up and reach out to do the same with hers. "CCTV once we're outside," I say. She pulls her scarf up over the lower part of her face. Our old clothes are in a locker on the ground floor, to be recovered another day.

She looks at me with liquid eyes. "What are we doing?"

"It'll be fine," I say. "In two hours it will all be over." We both know it's an empty reassurance.

The lift door slides open and we step out into the car park. The fluorescent lights are flickering, the pillars are painted a vivid red-orange, and the whole place is a hellscape, a migrainous horror of shifting light and colour. There's no sign of anyone else.

"What now?" Beatriz whispers.

I look at my watch. We're nearly half an hour early, and it's possible Ilya isn't here yet.

"Let's check row by row."

This floor of the car park is only about half full, and we carefully pick our way along. There's no one else around—if nothing else, it's a good place for a rendezvous.

"It's not too late to go home," I whisper.

Beatriz looks at me from under her hood. "And then what? We just have to get it over with."

A battered white Volkswagen Transporter van with red lettering—*Fontanero Garión 24/7*—flashes its lights at us. Slowly I walk towards it. The driver's door opens and Ilya slips out, a shorter man stepping down from the other side. They are both in black hoodies, but their hoods are down.

Ilya nods at the other guy. "Pavel."

Pavel looks back expressionlessly. His shaved head and stocky frame make me think I wouldn't want to tussle with him.

"You're early," says Ilya. "That's good. Get in the van. Turn your phones off."

"All four of us?"

"Pavel will ride in the back."

Pavel looks neither pleased nor displeased with this arrangement. He opens the back door and hops inside the cargo compartment.

I get in and sit next to Ilya and give my hand to Beatriz to help her up. She ignores it. If she appreciates my chivalry in sitting between her and a notorious gangster, she keeps it to herself.

Ilya starts up the engine, a rattly diesel. "So you, you have the keys, the codes?"

I've memorised the codes to be on the safe side. I'm hoping Beatriz has the keys. She gives a brisk nod without looking at Ilya.

"She's even brought her finger," I say. Nobody laughs. This isn't going to be one of those evenings we get through with gallows humour.

We pull out on to the motorway which is all but empty at this time of night. It sounds as if Ilya is having trouble with the clutch or the gearbox. Since I assume he's not a plumber in real life, this must be a stolen van, and I can't suppress a bleak grin at the irony of us breaking down. Although it won't be anything like as funny if it happens when we're getting away with the paintings.

Beatriz's gaze is fixed outside the window and I'm alone with my thoughts.

"What happens afterwards?" I say to Ilya.

"How do you mean?"

"Well, you and Pavel drive off with the loot—"

"'Loot'?

"The paintings. What about us?"

Ilya barks a sharp laugh. "What, you want a fucking taxi service?"

"It just doesn't seem a good idea to leave us in the Artesana, in case there are police."

Ilya tenses. "And why would there be police?"

I've got my own reasons for thinking there won't be, but you never know.

"Someone was suspicious enough to install fingerprint sensors at the last minute."

Ilya flicks us both a quick glance. "If there are police, there's no job. And you're dead. She's dead."

Beatriz flinches.

"Listen," I say. "We've done everything we were asked. It's not on us if you've fucked up the planning. Like stealing this piece of shit van."

I can see Ilya's knuckles whiten on the steering wheel. It's probably not a good idea to needle him.

"You think I am the top man? The big boss?" he says.

"I doubt it."

"Too fucking right, cowboy. I am lucky to stay alive myself if we don't get the 'loot'. You think I worry for two fucking seconds about you and the girl?"

Beatriz licks her dry lips next to me. "Let's just steal the paintings and forget about the police. No-one mentioned them when I registered for the fingerprint scanner. You, Ilya, take us in the van afterwards, drop us anywhere, and we never see you again."

Ilya frowned. "You told her my name?" he says to me.

"What, it's hardly your real name. Is it?"

Ilya says nothing. If he's the bright one, I'd love to see Pavel's Mensa application.

I'm trying to assess Beatriz's state of mind without being too obvious about it. From what I can see, she's in at least as good a state as me.

We slow down for traffic lights and the gearbox kicks again. If Ilya and Pavel can't even steal a van that works properly, how can I trust them to pull off an art heist? I begin to think that Beatriz and I might need to do more than punch the codes in. I've brought all this on myself, but to have got Beatriz involved in this... Too late for regrets now, and the alternatives are worse.

I touch her gently on the knee. "OK?" I mouth.

She shrugs and then nods. There's nothing I can do now if she's not.

Ilya turns on the radio. All Spanish stations sound the same to me, sickly third-rate Europop mangled even more by the van's tinny speakers. Beatriz, who is a much more serious muso than me, ignores it while Ilya taps his fingers on the steering wheel.

I see the hill of Montjuïc on the right. We're nearly there. I nudge Beatriz and point it out, and she responds with a listless nod. I briefly squeeze her hand but she pulls it away.

"Ready?" says Ilya. "Hoods up." He bangs on the partition behind him to alert Pavel.

We turn off Corts Catalans into Calàbria, then onto Consell de Cent. There's no sign of life. If the police are here they're keeping a low profile. I look at my watch—twenty past two.

The Galeria is in front of us. My stomach lurches as Ilya drives past, runs a red light, turns right onto Vildadomat. He coaxes the van's enormous turning circle to reverse into an on-street bay, ready for us to make a quick getaway—or at least as quick as the knackered Fontanero Garión van will allow.

He bangs twice on the panel behind him to alert Pavel. "Ready?"

"Yes," I say in as level a voice as I can manage. Beatriz just nods. She slides open the heavy van door and hops down. I'm right behind her.

The night is almost moonless, and I wonder whether to give Ilya credit for picking a naturally dark night. The streetlamps cast a pale white light, but there's no-one about anyway. Even in a city as nocturnal as Barcelona, Eixample in the small hours of Monday morning is not where it's happening.

Ilya and Pavel lead the way, their hooded forms a sinister presence on the street. They both pull on black gloves, Pavel also carrying a large black holdall. To the naked eye, Beatriz and I must look equally threatening. Luckily there's no-one around to see.

We're in front of the main doors. Ilya steps aside, gives Beatriz a gentle shove on the shoulder. "Open it."

Beatriz scrabbles in her pocket, brings out a small key which gleams in the streetlight. It slips out of her hand to bounce on the ground with a muffled clink. Pavel draws in a hissing breath.

"Sorry—"

I pick up the key while she's still apologising and hand it

back to her. She takes a deep breath, pushes it into the lock and turns.

There's a faint squeak and the glass case swings open to reveal the keypad. She looks across at me, as if somehow she needs my approval. I nod involuntarily and hope to God she remembers the code. Was it only a week ago a drunken Estel was pushing at this same pad? We hadn't thought to bring gloves but she pulls a tissue out of her pocket so her fingers don't touch the pad.

She doesn't hesitate: 3*1*0*5*9*0*

There's a *thunk* from the main glass doors in front of us—the locks retracting.

"We're in," Beatriz says in a monotone.

Ilya reaches out and pulls at the door handle with a gloved hand, and with a damp sucking sound the door opens. "Quick!" He beckons us through.

And we're standing in the foyer with the door closed behind us. A pale night lamp gives off the minimum of illumination for us to orient ourselves. I'm half-expecting an alarm to go off, but there's nothing. I have to stop myself from checking that the single CCTV camera in the foyer is still there—as long as my hood's up and I don't lift my head, it can't register my face.

Ilya cracks his knuckles with every appearance of satisfaction. "Open the main office, turn off the CCTV," he says to Beatriz.

She says nothing, strides across the foyer and pushes a code into another keypad. I follow her; there's nothing I can do to help except be in the moment with her.

She slips into the main office and I follow her. I don't know if she's been in here before but it's not obvious where the CCTV controls are. I bring out the tiny flashlight from my pocket and shine a narrow beam between my fingers.

"There," she whispers, pointing to a console at the back of

the office. I pick my way over. Even my Catalan is up to deciphering the switch reading *CCTV Activat/Desactivat*. Part of me wonders why they hadn't invested in a computer-activated system even as I push '*Desactivat*'.

I switch the flashlight off and go back out into the foyer.

"Done," says Beatriz.

There's only the main gallery itself now. A keypad, the fucking fingerprint sensor, and we're in.

Beatriz steps briskly forward. Ilya and Pavel barely need to be here. We could have done this ourselves.

She punches the keycode and lays her finger against the sensor. The indicator light flashes from red to green. She wipes the sensor with her tissue and tucks it back into her pocket.

"All yours," she says, her voice betraying the smallest shiver of fear.

"We'll wait out here," I say.

Ilya gives a frosty chuckle. "I don't think so, cowboy." He opens the door and steps through. Pavel, behind us, beckons us through.

I can't believe it's this easy. My ideas about heists come from films and TV. Where are the laser beams, the thieves winching themselves down from the ceiling in harnesses? This isn't much more involved than picking up a parcel from an Amazon locker.

The four of us step into the gallery where a week earlier Beatriz and I had been posing for photos in front of her artwork.

In front of us stands a security guard.

2

We all stare at each other in the dimly lit gallery. The guard is wearing a white shirt with black tie and trousers and has a short truncheon at his hip. But there's only one of him, and four of us. He isn't to know that Beatriz and I won't be any use in a fight.

The guard's hand drops uncertainly to the truncheon. I can hear Pavel's hissed indrawn breath, and out of the corner of my eye I see the faint light gleaming on Ilya's teeth. He hasn't even got his hood up and he's grinning.

"*Estar tranquilo*," he says softly. *Be calm.*

I look at Beatriz and put a finger to my lips. She's as tall as Pavel, dressed in shapeless clothes. If she doesn't say anything, the guard may not realise she's a woman. When the police investigate afterwards, there's no way we can let a witness put her at the scene.

The guard backs away, raises both hands.

Ilya reaches for the back of his waistband and pulls out a snub-nosed pistol. Pavel has dropped the holdall on the floor and already has a gun in his hand.

"Hey!" says the guard. He's got no further to back up. He's already against the wall.

"Did you know about this?" Ilya spits at us.

"Do you think we'd be here if we did?" I say and curse myself for speaking. My Spanish is good, but I know it has a Scottish accent. Let's hope the guard is too scared to pick up on it.

"Kill him," says Pavel.

"No!" screams Beatriz. So much for keeping her quiet. "You can't," she says more quietly, her voice shaking.

Whatever I thought we'd signed up for, this wasn't it. Pavel casually raises his pistol. I wonder if I am actually going to shit myself.

"No," says Ilya. "Too much noise."

"He's seen your face," says Pavel. "And heard the girl."

Ilya takes two steps forward to stand in front of the guard. His shirt has a badge reading *Enric, CIA Seguretat.* Ilya reaches out and rips it off with a single motion.

"I'm sure that—" he glances down at the badge in his hand "—Enric won't remember anything when the police talk to him. Not when he knows how easily we can find CIA Seguretat."

His voice has the quiet reasonableness I remember from that first night in Broadway. He's frightening me more than Pavel even though he's not the one threatening to use the pistol.

"I'm right, aren't I, Enric?" he says.

Enric's eyes are saucer-wide. He nods desperately.

"We can't do this," says Beatriz in a high voice. "We need to go."

Ilya shakes his head in a quick decisive motion. "He's already seen us. We might as well get what we've come for."

"I don't want anyone to get hurt."

I'm not sure this is the time to be arguing with Ilya, but what do I know?

Taking advantage of Ilya's distraction, Enric makes a run for the door, his rubber soles squeaking on the floor. Pavel tracks him with his pistol. I stick out a foot and Enric sprawls to the floor. I flap down on top of him. Looks like I've picked a side.

Enric struggles. "Calm the fuck down," I say. "I've just saved your fucking life."

"Get up," says Pavel, presumably to me because I've got Enric pinned under me. I'm not convinced he won't shoot both of us, so I scramble to my feet.

"Now?" says Pavel in a harsh voice.

"I said no." I think Ilya is the only one in the room in control of his emotions. "No killing unless we have to."

I could have done without the rider at the end, and I feel Beatriz flinch next to me.

"It seems like Enric isn't as clever as I'd thought." He steps forward and with a single rapid movement kicks Enric in the head. Enric crawls out of the way, Ilya follows and kicks him again: once, twice. Suddenly I think of Ignacio, his own head so badly injured he ended up in a coma. I wonder where Ilya was that night.

Beatriz clutches my arm and buries her head in my shoulder. I put both arms around her.

Enric is still crawling towards the door, some futile instinct overcoming even basic common sense. Ilya squats down in front of him. There are smears of blood on the floor. He takes Enric's head and tilts it up towards him.

"Can you hear me, Enric?"

Enric makes a whistling noise, blood bubbling through split lips, which Ilya takes for assent.

"If you tell the police any more than 'It was dark, I didn't see them properly', I will find you and I will kill you, and I will kill your family. Do you understand?"

Enric spits out a gobbet of bloody phlegm. "Yes."

"Are you sure, Enric of CIA Seguretat? Say if you aren't, and I can help you understand it even better."

Pavel sniggers from behind us.

"I—understand," gasps Enric. "I couldn't see you."

Ilya stands up and brushes dust from the floor off his gloves. "See? I knew you'd get it."

He makes a quick gesture to Pavel. "Keep your gun on him anyway. If he moves a millimetre towards the door, you can shoot him after all."

Pavel chuckles from inside his hood.

"Now," says Ilya, looking at Beatriz. "For the real business. Are there any more tricks we don't know about?"

"I don't know," she says miserably. "I'm nothing to do with the gallery."

"She's telling the truth," I say. "We're only part of the social club. We only knew about the fingerprint sensor because she had to register for it."

"Give me your torch."

I reach into my pocket. Ilya switches it on, examines the wall surrounding *The Adoration of the Magi*, presumably to see if it has a tripwire or a proximity sensor. He takes his time.

"There's normally nothing in here that's valuable," I say. "So if there's extra security it's only just been installed."

"Enric!" barks Ilya. "What other security is there?"

Enric coughs feebly. "I don't know. I was only told to stay here all night, call the police if there was a problem."

Ilya gingerly lifts the bottom an inch or so from the wall and shines the flashlight into the gap. "It looks like just a normal hanging," he says.

"Hurry up!" says Pavel, twitching.

"Your pal needs his fix," I say. "He's going cold turkey."

Ilya gently puts the painting back in position and steps

across to me with silent menace. "You have a lot to say now, cowboy."

"Enough," says Beatriz. "I know about hanging paintings. I've organised exhibitions. If you shine the torch up, I can see if there are any extra wires."

Ilya nods and grins. "Good. Do it. Your girlfriend has more balls than you."

I assume this is directed at me.

"I'm not his girlfriend," says Beatriz.

Ilya laughs. "He just follows your pussy, hey? Is that right, cowboy?"

The only thing I can say is nothing. Ilya has to be the alpha male, and since he has a gun and a henchman, it seems sensible to let him.

Beatriz has finished her inspection. "There are no extra wires. And this painting is the most famous and the most valuable. So if it's clear, all the others will be too."

Ilya ponders this for a moment and nods. "OK. Cowboy, you get the bag."

Pavel picks it up and slides it across the floor to me.

"You, girl," Ilya says. "You know how to unhook the paintings quickly?"

She nods.

"OK. You do it, we put them in the bag and we're out of here."

I jerk my head towards Enric. "And him?"

"You think he's gonna talk to the cops?"

"No."

"Good. Because if you think that, I kill him." He gives Enric a werewolf grin in the night.

He claps his hands at Beatriz. "Come on, we haven't got all night."

We probably have, I think, but I'd rather be out of here too. I open the bag to its maximum extent and slide in *The Adoration of the Magi.*

From the edge of the room, Enric groans. Beatriz steps away from the second picture and walks over to him.

"Lie still," she says, kneeling next to him. "Let me see what is wrong with you."

"Carry on with the pictures," snaps Ilya.

"He's hurt!" Beatriz fires back. "Thanks to you."

"Beatriz—" Nothing good is going to come of this.

She takes the tissue out her pocket and wipes blood from Enric's face.

"I said, take the pictures down." There's a tightness in Ilya's voice that hasn't been there before. He doesn't need either of us any more now we're inside the main gallery. I wonder if Beatriz has worked that out.

"Do you want him to die? A murder investigation?"

However injured Enric is, I don't know what Beatriz can do to save him. But I understand that she can't leave him to lie in his own blood.

"I'll take the pictures down," I say. "We know they aren't wired."

"Yeah, do the woman's job," sniggers Pavel.

Coming from the guy who won't pick his arse without Ilya's say-so, this is rich, but he's not worth the argument. And he's not the one who's going to stop us getting out of the room safely, even if he does have a gun.

Gingerly I unhook one of the paintings. The fixing is more complex than I'd expected but eventually I get there. I put it into the bag and move on to the next one.

Ilya paces up and down the gallery, his gun lost in his giant hands. "This would go quicker with two of us, pal," I say. I'd rather he's pissed off with me than Beatriz.

He stalks over to me, lifts the top of my hood with one hand

and looks into my face. He makes a sudden motion with his gun hand, just inside my peripheral vision. I flinch, and he laughs. "Just take down the fucking pictures."

Our best way out of here is to stop the situation escalating. Enric's appearance—and Ilya kicking the shit out of him—hasn't really helped, but the key is to keep Ilya as calm as possible. His restraint at the moment is frightening in itself, but under the surface there's very little keeping the violence at bay. For now, I've taken his attention away from Beatriz and that's enough. I'm long past the idea that I can protect her if this goes tits up. The best I can do is share her fate, but I can't change it. I go back to unclipping the pictures.

From the other side of the room, Beatriz says quietly: "He needs an ambulance." Enric's head is lolling against her thigh. I'm not sure if he's fully conscious.

"Yeah, call 112," says Pavel. "You can get the police as well."

"Shut the fuck up," says Ilya.

"He's not very bright, is he?" I say. It's worth trying to set them against each other. Ilya casually backhands me in the face. It's his gun hand and it feels like I've been hit by a train.

"Tomàs!" cries Beatriz.

"I'm fine." I can feel blood trickling from my nose.

"Both of you," says Ilya in a low voice. "Understand—no ambulance, no chat. We take the pictures, we get in the van, we go."

"And him?" Beatriz nods down at Enric.

Ilya shrugs. "He lives, he dies. God decides."

This probably isn't the time for a debate on fatalism, so I wipe the blood off my lip with the back of my hand and get back to unhooking pictures.

Eventually we're done. Six paintings in the bag, Enric slumped unconscious against Beatriz, Pavel covering them both with his gun, and Ilya surveying the scene with a negligent superiority. Beatriz still has her hood up and I can't catch her eye. It's not impossible they'll kill us at this point, I realise. Probably not—a murdered foreigner and a pretty middle-class girl might prompt an unusually thorough investigation—but it's not out of the question. Ilya isn't motivated by sentiment.

"Give him the bag." Ilya points at Pavel, who puts his gun away. "Now, we walk out of here, quickly to the van, hoods up. Same seats as on the way here."

Beatriz gently lays Enric on the ground in the recovery position. "And him?"

"Fuck, woman! Once we're away from the gallery, you and pussy-boy can get out. Call an ambulance from a call box. Don't switch your mobiles on until tomorrow morning."

Beatriz looks out from under her hood. "*Bé*."

It's the best we're going to do. I pray that she's not going to kick off over it. I wish Enric all the best—the poor sod's just in the wrong place at the wrong time—but all I'm concerned with is getting Beatriz and me out of here safely.

Pavel, bag in one hand, opens the door to the foyer and steps through, followed by me, Beatriz and, at the rear with his gun on us, Ilya. I'm half-expecting the police to be there—can we really have turned off the CCTV without alerting someone? — but it's empty. On soft feet we bustle across to the front door and freedom.

3

WE SCURRY ALONG THE STREET UNDER THE FLICKERING LIGHTS, turning right to find the Fontanero Garión van still parked outside the school. Ilya presses the remote to unlock, and Pavel opens the rear doors and hops into the back with the paintings. The rest of us take up the same seats as on the way here.

The engine rattles but at least it fires first time. The middle seat in the front has a lap belt, which I didn't bother with on the first journey, and now can't adjust to fit me. Beatriz calmly buckles her own seatbelt.

Ilya pulls out onto the empty street. This part of the city is a nightmarish one-way system. I've never driven here and I don't envy Ilya trying to find his way back out.

Beatriz has her eyes locked on the passenger wing mirror, alert for anything which might be coming up behind us. Trapped in the middle, I can see nothing except what's directly ahead. We turn onto Corts Catalanes, and for a moment I almost admire Ilya: he's going to take us out past police HQ. After that, the road to the motorway is clear. I wonder where he's planning to drop us, and I don't give much for Enric's hopes of a speedy ambulance.

Beatriz knows the city inside out and she's more alert to it than I am. "Let us go," she says. "There's a metro station ahead. We can disappear into that."

"Sorry," grins Ilya, who's in no way sorry. "I'll find a service station on the motorway. Buy yourselves some breakfast and call a taxi."

"But the guard—"

Ilya takes his eyes off the road for long enough to stare Beatriz down.

We pull up at traffic lights ahead of a crossroads. There's a car behind us, and two either side of the junction. They have the green light, but they stop in the middle of the road. Blocking us in. Blocking us in—this isn't accidental.

Ilya swears, snaps the headlight on full beam and tries to turn the van in the road. But we're stationary at the traffic lights and the engine protests, accompanied by the grinding of the gearbox.

"You told them!" he hisses across at us. "You spoke to the police!"

Now isn't the time to mention that, yes I did, but I told them the wrong date. They should be here, right enough—but this time tomorrow, not now. Is Rosell in one of the unmarked cars?

The two cars at the junction pull in behind us. The one in front tries to block us. Ilya floors the accelerator, Beatriz screams, and I remember that I'm not wearing a seatbelt. The van accelerates from a standing start like an arthritic elephant, straight at the car in front. I brace my legs against the dashboard, but if there's a head-on impact I'm going straight through the windscreen.

At the last moment Ilya swerves aside, the van responding with a spongy wallow. The passenger side clips the police car, ripping the wing mirror free. Beatriz scrabbles towards me, as far from the door as she can get. In the back, Pavel is bellowing.

We're past the police car, but doing maybe forty k.p.h. in second gear, and against the flow of a one-way street. Our long-term prospects are not encouraging. Ilya roars as he fights with the clutch, but he can't get the van into third. The slowest police chase since OJ Simpson.

The two cars behind us have put red and blue flashing lights on, but they're not bothering with sirens. One overtakes us in the parallel lane, obviously to block us from the front. There's a gun in Ilya's hand.

If this turns into a gunfight, no-one's going to know that Beatriz and I are the good guys. We're every bit as likely as Ilya to get shot.

As the cop car pulls level with us, Ilya raises his left arm. I sprawl on top of him, free from the restraint of a seatbelt. Ilya's arm drops, there's a huge explosion in the cramped space and a side window disintegrates. The force of my jump pushes Ilya against the door, and he can't get his gun arm up to get off another shot.

Neither can he steer the van. Beatriz is screaming, screaming as we lurch away from the police car, across the central reservation. We plunge off the road, onto the pavement. I see a neon sign—*Rock 'n' Roll All Night*—then nothing, a bang, and when I look up, I'm lying on the van bonnet, clouds of steam rising around me.

We're half-inside a takeaway which the van has largely demolished. Beatriz manages to force the passenger door open and slide out. Ilya isn't so lucky: the driver's door is jammed and it doesn't occur to him to slide across and follow Beatriz out.

She's leaning across me on the bonnet. "Tomàs! Talk to me! Tomàs!"

I gingerly lift my head. I can feel pebbles of broken windscreen glass under my hands. "I'm OK," I say, and reach out my hand towards her.

"*Ningú es mou!*" shouts a voice. *Nobody move.* My options are pretty limited anyway, and it doesn't look like Beatriz is going anywhere. In seconds we're surrounded by cops in Special Intervention Group bullet-proof vests, some with pistols, some with machine guns. They're all pointed at us—although they seem much more interested in Ilya, still thrashing in the cockpit of the van, than they are in Beatriz.

"There's one in the back!" I shout. "He's got a gun."

I try to roll off the bonnet to test how badly hurt I am, but immediately there's a machine pistol in my ribs. I take it they're happy with me where I am.

I can't see the back of the van, but the doors are levered open and soon Pavel is dragged out, his pistol lying on the ground in front of him. I wonder whether Ilya is the sort to go down in a hail of bullets, but after some shouted instructions he ejects the magazine, throws it out of the van, and then the pistol.

Two cops reach into the cockpit and pull him out. He stands unsteadily, a cut on his forehead, as the police put on handcuffs. He gives Beatriz and me a stare with as much menace and malevolence as he has left.

And that's the heist we spent six months planning - over. I've not managed to keep myself out of it, and worst of all, Beatriz is here too, blank-faced under the guns.

It's over. Everything's as fucked as it can possibly be. This surely can't get any worse.

Another unmarked car, lights flashing, screeches to a halt outside the wrecked takeaway. One of the doors open and a man in plain clothes scrambles out. He pulls a warrant card from his pocket, holds it up.

"All of you get back," he says. "I need to talk to the prisoners."

It's Aleix.

4

I HAVE ANOTHER GO AT STANDING UP. I DON'T SEEM TO BE TOO BADLY hurt, although Beatriz takes hold of one arm to make sure I don't topple over.

"Aleix? What the fuck?"

He gives an apologetic smile. "Sorry. I should probably have mentioned at some point that I'm a detective, but it was never the right time."

"Beatriz? Did you—"

She just shakes her head dumbly.

Out of the corner of my eye I can see Ilya and Pavel being bundled into a police van. A uniformed officer wanders over. "Shall I take these two, sir?"

Aleix shakes his head. "Call for another van. I don't want these two with the Russians. I need to talk to them first, anyway."

"You're sure?"

Aleix pats a pistol at his hip. "I'm sure. The rest of you can go."

Two other cops finish taping off the getaway van as a crime

scene. The others are dispersing the small crowd watching events unfold.

There's a bench in the central reservation under the garish glare of a streetlight. Aleix leads us across and we sit down. He remains standing with his back against the lamppost.

I try to take Beatriz's hand but she moves it away.

"Aleix," she says. "There's guard at the Artesana. They attacked him, he's hurt."

"We've got a team on the way there," he says. "He'll be in the best hands."

The three of us look around at each other, wondering what next.

"Well, this is a shitshow," says Aleix.

"Yeah," I say. "Sorry to have inconvenienced you and all. Maybe if you'd told us you were a cop..."

"Were you watching us all along, Aleix?" says Beatriz in a level tone. The streetlight casts black shadows under her eyes. "Did you know about this all summer?"

Aleix scratches his stubble. "You think I'd have let Tommy play you if I'd known what was happening? The first I knew was yesterday."

A guy in an apron wanders over from the wrecked takeaway with three coffees. At least their kitchen is still working.

"You're really a cop?" I say.

"Yeah. I'm really a cop. Detective seconded to ACCO. And I always liked you, Tommy, and I still do in a way, but I'm sending you to jail."

I gesture towards the taped-off van. "It's not quite what it looks. And Beatriz is only here under duress."

"I'd guessed that." He gives Beatriz something that's trying to be a reassuring smile.

"How did you know about this, Aleix?" she says.

"Every cop's greatest friend, luck. I was in the office on

Friday when a cop I don't know comes in to talk to my boss with information that there's a robbery planned on the Artesana."

"Rosell," I say.

"That's him. Says he's had an anonymous tip that he's inclined to believe. I'm not even really listening, I've got enough work of my own, and then I hear a name I recognise: Thomas Chisholm."

"Once heard, never forgotten," I mutter.

"And so I go over, say I know you, and then I'm on the case. Rosell tells me what he knows, he reckons it's linked to the Russians because of this guy Ignacio Fuentes. And then he mentions you, Beatriz. And I know that no way are you involved with underworld criminals."

"You were wrong, then," she says with an acid side-glance at me.

"I knew straight away that it was all Tommy. How he'd been chasing you all year, and now I could see why."

"It wasn't just—" But no-one's interested in what I have to say any more.

"Rosell thought the tip-off was sound and so did I. I thought maybe you had a conscience about it, Tommy. But even that was wrong, wasn't it? Because that evening I got a text from Estel. To say we all needed to provide an alibi for you and Beatriz, no questions asked. For us to meet at El Gat Blau and say the pair of you were there. And then I knew the robbery wasn't tomorrow, it's tonight. And that you weren't helping us, you were throwing us off the scent."

He chuckles. "Estel's probably still there now, wondering where the fuck I am. We're going to need a chat later about false alibis."

"For fuck's sake, Aleix!" I shout. "She's only doing it to protect Beatriz!"

"And you care about them both so much." For the first time I see the cop in him.

I stand and try to face him down. "This is nothing to do with Estel, nothing to do with Beatriz. You have me, I can't deny it. But Estel, Beatriz? They're innocent."

He looks at Beatriz. "They're not, though, are they? Beatriz has actually taken part in the robbery, Estel is part of the conspiracy."

"So how much are you going to let go?"

"'Let go'? They're my friends, but I'm a cop. It's the law and this is my job."

I'm an inch away from his face. "You have nothing on Estel, and Beatriz has a viable defence. Do you really want to make them testify against the Russians? From everything I hear about this city, that's not a good idea."

Beatriz reaches up to put a hand on my arm. "It's not Aleix's fault."

The remark falls into the sticky night air because we all know whose fault it is.

I'd like to pretend what happens next is unvarnished selflessness on my part, but the fact is, I've no way out of this at all. *Zugzwang.*

I sit back down. "OK, Aleix. How's this? You've got two Russians at the scene. I assume they won't plead guilty or say anything at all unless they want to turn up dead in their cells one morning."

"They never talk," says Aleix.

"I'll talk. Plead guilty, give you the person who set me up with the Russians." *Because you deserve to go down with the rest of us, Hannah.* "There might be holes in the story but it gets a conviction. Who's going to look too closely?"

Aleix gives a bitter laugh. "You might want to talk to a

lawyer before you do that. I'm saying that as a friend—a former friend—and not a cop."

"There's a price for my testimony."

"Fuck you, Tommy. You think you're getting immunity? You wouldn't live long to enjoy it."

"The price is," I say with as much dignity as I can muster, "Beatriz's name disappears from the record. You don't book her; you make it right with your colleagues. You know as well as I do that she's only here now because I conned her. You're not letting a criminal go."

Aleix nods. "Go on."

"And because I'm not an idiot, yes, you put me in witness protection. A new identity. My testimony can't take down the Russians, although Hannah Layton's can, but they're not going to be too chuffed with me. I think maybe I deserve a reduced sentence for that, but it's not up to me."

Beatriz's eyes are glistening in the light. "You don't have to..."

"Of course I do. You know what I've done to you, B. This doesn't make any of that better, but at least it stops you being washed away with all the rest."

Aleix drains his coffee cup and drops it on the ground. "I don't get the final say on this, but I'll recommend to my boss that we agree. The paintings are recovered, two Russian thugs in jail, a conviction, and a way into the bigger fish. It's a win."

I see a police van coming towards us.

"So, I get in the van with you, and Beatriz goes home." I look across the road to the metro station and hold out my hand to Aleix. He takes it and shakes.

"Can you give me a minute with Beatriz?" I say. "I'm not going to run off."

He nods and raises his hand to the cop driving the van.

. . .

Beatriz and I are sitting on the bench. "So. This is it," I say. "It's all over, the worst has happened. I don't know when—if—I'll ever see you again. All I can do is say sorry. I never meant for any of this to happen."

She takes my face in her hands. Her eyes are full of unshed tears. "I know," she says softly. "I almost don't blame you. Almost."

"Can you forgive me, at least?"

She kisses my cheek. "I could never hate you, Tomàs."

I touch her hair. "You know, if they put me in witness protection, it's a new identity, a new life. We won't be able to contact each other. Whether I go to prison or not, you won't know who I am."

She smiles sadly. "I never knew who you were, Tomàs."

I stand up, take her hand. "It was all real, you know. I loved you. I still do."

She draws away and looks into my face. She's openly crying now and she reaches into her pocket for her tissue. But that's back at the Artesana sodden with Enric's blood. She wipes her eyes with her sleeve instead.

"And I love you. But I can never trust you. I deserve better."

I kiss her one last time. "Yes, Beatriz. You do."

I swing away from her and walk towards Aleix. As he puts the cuffs on my wrists, Beatriz raises a hand in sad salute and turns towards the metro station.

EPILOGUE

MARCH 2016

How Will I Find You?

We aren't that busy, so I'm wiping the tables down before the evening rush starts. Cafè Amfiteatre is nothing if not clean.

"You want to take your break, Ramón?" calls Sofia from behind the bar.

"Sure," I say. The evening is beginning to cool, and all three outside tables are empty.

I pick the one farthest from the door, light a cigarette and get my phone out to check my emails. From inside I hear the hiss of the coffee machine. Sofia may not pay much, but I'm always kept caffeinated. And when, as night draws in, her face is caught in shadows, sometimes she reminds me of... but we won't go there.

Nothing worthwhile in my emails, of course, although I'm at a point in life where no news is good news. I check my old Chisholm address, just out of completeness, but there's only spam there today. Polly dropped me as a client long ago, of course, but I eventually repaid the advance and even managed to sell the fantasy novel to a small press. Somehow I managed to lose money on that.

Sometimes there's an email from Aleix, but not today. I know the convictions from the Artesana heist have made his career—Hannah ratted on the Russian bosses and most of them in are jail now—but I never expected him to keep in touch. It's almost as if he remembers the time we were friends with affection. He doesn't know my new identity, and he thinks I've been resettled in Málaga. He'd have kittens if he knew I was in Tarragona, only an hour outside Barcelona. But somehow I can't keep away.

Aleix's emails are the only link I have left with the old days. When I was set up with the new identity I was advised to stay away from Barcelona, and I have. I don't think there's anyone there now who'd want to see me anyway. Aleix keeps me up to date with what the crew are up to. Estel has a small but regular part in a Spanish soap opera which I watch occasionally to get a glimpse of her. Beatriz had her big exhibition in the Petritxol, and a couple of others since. She's not hit the big time yet, but she's getting there. Aleix doesn't tell me if she has a boyfriend, and I don't ask.

Sofia brings the coffee over, her long white apron belted tight to accentuate her waist.

"Anything interesting?" she says, indicating my phone.

"Is there ever?" I laugh.

"Back to work in five, then."

She smiles and kisses the top of my head. I'm not sure what our relationship is, but it suits both of us for now. She doesn't ask about my past; since I'm not allowed to tell her about witness protection and I've resolved not to lie to her, that's the only way it can work. And if I have any questions about why someone so intelligent and educated is running a marginal backstreet bar in Tarragona, I keep those to myself too. If she remembers me coming in a couple of years ago with someone else, she's never said so. One day we'll reach double or quits time, but I don't think either of us is in a hurry to get there.

I finish my coffee in a single gulp and stand up to go back inside. No doubt the toilets could do with another clean.

As I leave the table I look back over my shoulder. On the hill a few miles down the coast I see the sun setting over the Castell de Claramunt, where a long time ago I was someone else, and happy.

ACKNOWLEDGMENTS

It's possible to write a novel without help from anyone. It's called a first draft, and will remain unpublished and unpublishable.

My peerless beta readers and support group ensured that didn't happen with *Catfish Alley.* Aliya Whiteley read not only the first but several subsequent drafts, and identified plot holes that would have sunk the novel. I'm also grateful for helpful observations and encouragement from Roger Morris, Anna Legat, and Steve Sherman.

Over fifteen years ago, Macmillan New Writing launched several writing careers, including mine. I've been immensely grateful for the support from my fellow writers from that cohort: Elizabeth Graham, Alis Hawkins, Roger Morris, Frances Stott, Deborah Swift, Len Tyler and Aliya Whiteley.

My publisher SpellBound Books believed in *Catfish Alley* when nobody else did. I'm especially grateful to Sumaira Wilson for taking a chance on it, and Nikki East for editing (and the fabulous cover design).

My stepdaughter Danielle Fleet is a Chisholm by birth, although her character bears no resemblance to her namesake Tommy. I'm glad at last to have written a novel she wants to read.

In the book, Tommy and Beatriz often communicate through their shared musical tastes. All the songs in *Catfish Alley* are on the official Spotify playlist if you want to get into the mood:

https://open.spotify.com/playlist/5O10SjnIuobqDICzSWBh7P?si=e219d50455ab4753

If you've enjoyed the book, I'd love it if you left a review on Amazon. It doesn't have to be long, but it will help other readers discover the book. Thanks in advance!

Printed in Great Britain
by Amazon